DOUBLE-SIDED MAGIC

(LEGACY SERIES BOOK 1)

MCKENZIE HUNTER

This is a work of fiction. Names, characters, businesses, places, events, and incidents are either the products of the author's imagination or used in a fictitious manner. Any resemblance to actual persons, living or dead, or actual events is purely coincidental.

McKenzie Hunter

Double-Sided Magic

© 2016, McKenzie Hunter

mckenziehunter.author@gmail.com

ISBN: 978-1-946457-99-8

ACKNOWLEDGMENTS

With each book I am always humbled by the number of people who take the time out of their schedule to make this possible. First, I would like to thank my mother and friends: Sheryl Cox-Weber, Stacy McCright, April Franklin, Marcia Snyder, and Tiffany Dix, who are always supportive and find time to help me whenever I ask. Hugs and a million thanks to my wonderful beta readers: Angie "Nana" Hatcher, Kathy Beard, Kylie Kniese, Marla Maslan, Misty Chancellor, Vanessa Jorgensen, and Ryan Sundy.

I would also like to give a special thanks to Luann Reed-Siegel, my editor, and Orina Kafe, my wonderful and gifted cover artist.

Last but definitely not least, I would like to thank my readers for giving my book a chance.

CHAPTER 1

I thought he hadn't seen me, but when his pace quickened behind me, I knew it wasn't a coincidence. He had been following me for two days. *Tracker.* I cursed under my breath and picked up the pace, jogging past other runners on the trail, moving in the opposite direction. *Damn Tracker.* My jog soon became a slow run, fast enough to get away from the crowd but slow enough not to alarm anyone hopped up on an endorphin high. I veered off the trail into the uneven, thick forest. The smell of oak and flowering dogwood coated the area, and dirt that kicked up into a small dust wouldn't help mask my scent. Shifters—the best hunters. I kept going, running around the trees, never in a straight line in case he decided to use a gun. My heart racing, I kept my pace. Added to my typical five miles were the ten more I needed to get to the spot. He wouldn't tire—which was good. I wanted him to continue—I was going to end it.

His pace quickened behind me, closing the distance I had. Skilled lithe steps followed me as I led him deeper into the bosk, away from witnesses staying on the trail. And he was more than happy to oblige and confront me without witnesses. We both needed to be away from prying eyes. He needed it to fulfill his job and murder me; I needed it to make sure he failed.

If he attacked in public, he would be considered a rogue shapeshifter who attacked a helpless human in the park while she was jogging. And that was exactly what I was to the rest of the world, an average human woman running in the park. I played my role well. That was the way it had to be if I planned to stay alive.

The rest of the world considered us extinct, destroyed—nothing more than a tale of powerful magic gone bad. People who deserved to die, given their justice for what they did, and I couldn't say they were wrong. There was no redemption, and we didn't deserve mercy. I got it. All the bloodshed couldn't erase what my kind had done. We were the embellished stories of how strong power made people hunger for more. Our story became a cautionary tale. We were the boogeyman; a historical account of how magic could destroy. How the allure of it could corrupt, and there was such a thing as *too much* magic. I was too much magic. Raw magic, strong magic—deadly magic. Being all that, it seemed as though I should be the hunter, not the hunted.

Magic wasn't all bad; fae, shifters, mages, and witches weren't problems. They were the safe zone. Me and my kind —we were "kill on sight." And that's exactly what they did to my parents. There was a different ache in my heart, unlike the usual one I felt when I ran this long and hard. Tears welled; I blinked them back. I inhaled the crisp, refreshing air, potent with oak and poplar, and I pushed harder, only a few miles to go.

I kept running into the thicket, fully aware he would follow me no matter where I went. The tenacity of Trackers. They were the conspiracy theorists of the world, made up of a small group of mages, shifters, fae, and humans. Everyone else believed we had been wiped out, and they needed to—because if not, they'd live in fear. Trackers didn't, and they were prepared to remedy that. I wasn't sure how they found us. I suspected they were always there in the shadows, cynical about my kind, just waiting for us to screw up and show that we were too dangerous to live so they could justify eliminating us. We'd certainly proven them right in the past —in a big way.

I didn't know how they kept track of us now. I'd once imagined a complicated system, but I'd come to believe it was more like a group of misfits meeting in basements to share binders of papers that traced our bloodlines, scrolls about our lineage, and Post-it notes about possible sightings. They were probably the guys who told tall tales of spotting Bigfoot. The world considered them crazy and innocuous. We considered them deadly—and they were.

It had been a year since one had come after me. He'd been a mage, easier to trap, harder to fight. This one was a shifter —he would be harder to fight but easier to stop, an innately skilled hunter—and based on the way he moved, a wolf.

I got enough distance, getting a glimpse of the patch of missing grass that indicated a small pit cave that had been made by someone and thankfully forgotten. It had become my refuge since I'd stumbled upon it a little over two years ago. I sprinted toward it, opened the cover of my clandestine hideaway, and lowered myself into it, aware that he would follow.

The smell of dirt, stone, and wood from the retention wall surrounded me, and I squinted, trying to adjust to the darkness. The hint of magic, like the dirt, kicked up in the air and reminded me that I had to hide mine and this was my only safe place where I could use it. I'd placed a ward on it, the magic often masked by other magic that inundated the area. I'd used it without problems, so I assumed it was safe—

or as safe as it could be. The benefit of being considered extinct was that most people couldn't identify our magic, because they hadn't been exposed to it enough. If they felt it, they would assume it was an area where witches, fae, and mages had used magic.

I stepped farther back; light streamed from above, where I'd left the cover open. As a predator, he had the advantage of heightened sense of smell and vision. This was the first time I'd had a shifter after me. Taking several controlled breaths, I waited for him, pressed against the reinforced wall, the hardened dirt biting into my skin. Fear was a lingering fragrance in the air. It was taking too long. I knew he knew where I was. Maybe he wouldn't follow. I waited. Crouching in the corner, I waited for him to drop down. For moments there wasn't anything but silence, and then he leapt down.

I was without my weapons but here I could use magic undetected. Using it in front of humans wasn't the issue. As far as they were concerned, I was just one of the many magical beings that populated the city. It was the supernaturals that I worried about, because they could sense the "different" magic. If they were skilled enough, they would know the difference, or at least know that my magic wasn't fae, witch, or mage. All it would take was one spell. They'd feel it against their skin, the roil of it over the body, the potency of power, and there would be no denying that I wasn't just one of the typical magical beings. They could sense it in the air, but if magic had been performed or another supernatural was in the vicinity, it could distort it. Shifters were a different story. It was rumored they could smell magic. I wasn't sure just how they perceived magic, which is why I kept my distance from them.

"Only the guilty run," said his deep voice as he dropped down into the pit. A small halo of light formed around him as he looked around the dark cavity. His pale features dimmed, but his effervescent green eyes were bright enough to see in the dusky surroundings. His nose flared as he took in my scent, and his narrowed eyes scanned the area. The list of things that were easier than fighting a shifter was pretty long and included climbing Mount Everest. I would need magic. His hands were placed on the hilt of his knife as he approached me.

"Anya." He said my name with the familiarity of a friend. But if he was as thorough and psychotic as Trackers were known to be, he probably knew me as well as his friends. And he also knew that I didn't go by Anya. To my parents I was Anya; to the world who knew me as the human who collected old things in the quaint little antique shop in Manor Square, I was Olivia Michaels—Levy.

The strike that sent me into the wall of the pit was enough to startle me into defense mode. To most supernaturals, fighting a shifter, if you weren't skilled in some form of combat, was a death sentence, because they were immune to all magic. Which was why they really hated us—they weren't immune to ours. His hand shot out again; I blocked it. I wasn't going to get him on speed and strength. He had me on that. I dropped down and swiped his leg. The moment he hit the ground, my elbow slammed into his windpipe. He choked in a sharp breath and blocked me from doing it again. He recovered, a little faster than I expected. I came to my feet, a side kick landing a hard jolt to his nose. It should have stopped the bastard. Wolves. I never understood why they of all shifters were drawn to living in packs. They were resilient and obstinate enough to fight until they were the last man standing.

Eyes glassy with unshed tears, I moved just in time to miss his foot as it kicked out. It didn't catch me square on the shoulder, but clipped it, and it hurt like hell. "You will not leave here alive," he said. Before the second kick sent me careening into the wall again, my head snapped back into his. A spiral of colors flashed before my eyes; the pain unfolded and built into something that was barely tolerable. It was hard to shake it off. But I had to, because he charged at me. I moved in time, my palm thrusting into the side of his temple, dazing him.

"If you're after me, then you know who I am. The bigger concern is whether or not *you* will get out of here alive." Magic that I forced to stay dormant rose slowly in me, wrapping around me like a heavy blanket but offering me no comfort. Used so infrequently for fear of being discovered, it felt foreign to me. But I needed it more than just for defense, so I took a few minutes to become familiar with it again. To own it the way my parents had taught me. To become one with it until the vibrant glow of amber, blue, and white was just an extension of me like my limbs. It shot out, fastening him against the wall. His arms and legs pressed firmly against it. I started to remove his weapons. His body might not have been able to move, but the clenched jaw and ire in his eyes as he glared at me were enough to scare someone who hadn't seen the things that I had. When I was finished, I looked at the small pile of blades, guns, vials of salt, and iridium cuff. We didn't have many weaknesses, but like any magical being, we had one. Shifters had silver. Fae, witches, and mages were allergic to iron. It took iridium to disable us, reduce our magic to something that could be bested by the weakest of witches. I glanced at the cuff: it wasn't thick enough. It wasn't enough to stop me.

"I will find you again, you can bet on that."

And I knew if he had a chance he would. This was the second time one had found me in two years. Was it time to move again? I'd been here for so long. This was my home. I liked my job, my employer, my roommate. How long would I have to keep paying for the sins of people I didn't know?

Whose beliefs I didn't share and whose thirst for power I didn't possess. I was bound to them for one reason only—my magical ability. The anger started to rise in me, along with the same frustration that surfaced each time I thought about it. I didn't need anger. This needed to be handled with a steady hand and level head.

"You are either really arrogant or really stupid. Here I am with a stack of blades, your blades, and only one person to test out their sharpness on, and you're talking BS." The glare didn't ease, his sharp features rigid. He pulled his mouth back as though he would expose fangs. It was easy to suspect that he was one who was more comfortable in his animal form.

I picked up a knife and examined the blade, my finger running across it as I stared at him. The anger started boiling to the surface again, ready to spread to a forest fire. It was people like him that left me alone—orphaned—by the age of fifteen because my parents were killed. I gripped the handle harder. The anger was roaring. I was having a hard time trying to control it. I needed to be under control more than ever. I didn't kill. I was better than that. *I don't kill, I'm better than that.* I repeated that mantra over and over until I accepted it. If I killed, I wouldn't be better than the people who'd forced me into this life where I had to lie and hide to survive.

The brush of sympathy reasserted itself. He had every right to want me dead and ensure that I didn't exist. The acts of a few warranted a full-out effort to destroy us so that we could never cause the level of devastation that we had in the past. I understood, but I couldn't change who and what I was.

I whispered the incantation. The words gently flowed from me as though I was in the warded cave with my mother, practicing our forbidden magic so that I wouldn't be defenseless in a world that wanted me dead. The magic

7

cloaked me, twirling around my arm, and danced across my finger.

"Don't you touch me," he barked. The magic would hurt his pride more than anything. Immune to all other magic, shifters possessed a certain level of arrogance about it.

"It'll only hurt for a moment."

He growled, attempted to thrash against the hold. He was strong—each time he railed against the hold, it felt like something slammed into me. I stepped closer. He gritted his teeth and bared them in silence when I slashed the knife across his arm. I waved my hand over the pool of blood that welled from the cut. He finally relaxed back with quiet resolve as the magic mixed with his blood, the tranquil allure of it slowly taking over and my magic traipsing through it, grabbing pieces of his memory and replacing them with false ones. He wouldn't look for me again. I closed my eyes, concentrating, pulling the ones I needed and replacing them with others. Giving a nice neat timeline where he tracked me into the cave, lively banter, before he used his dagger to stab me. He would remember watching me struggle for breath, grapple with that idea that I was going to die. And then the comfort of knowing he watched me struggle and succumb to death. He would feel the very real satisfaction of watching a Legacy die.

I slumped against the wall across from him, exhausted. It was easier to use my magic and implant memories in a shifter, who didn't possess magic, than use it on those who did. Humans were absolutely easy, but they weren't used in the field, only for reconnaissance and research. Waiting for the exhaustion to pass, I reveled in small favors. I couldn't get this far with the mage who had come after me—his magic was too strong to lift more than part of his memory, which was probably why someone was after me again.

The area was still deserted, but I would have to move

quickly. It wasn't on the trail, but every once in a while someone would wander along it.

I am going to feel this tomorrow, I thought. I carried the shifter up the small stairs leading out of the pit cave. He felt like solid, dense muscle. I was too exhausted to use magic to lift him. This wasn't the best trade-off for being able to use magic against him. Even using a fireman's carry was difficult. Implanting false memories took a lot out of me, but I didn't want to risk keeping him in the cave and moving him later. I ignored the pulse of pain that shot through my shoulder and positioned him against a tree and replaced his weapons on him.

Maybe this was the last time they would come for me.

I was glad I had just missed my roommate. Exhausted, I barely made it back to the apartment; I didn't have it in me to come up with a believable lie to explain the bruising and torn and dirty clothing. Instead of a shower, I stood in the middle of the steam-filled bathroom trying to think of what to do next. Two Trackers in a year. In the past ten years, I'd only had three come after me. That was a lot. I didn't want to move again and change things. I liked my home—my life.

CHAPTER 2

*K*alen's smile mirrored my scowl as the magic wrapped around the tips of his fingers. I waited for him to make a move. He dismissed my glare, and when my hand balled at my side, he laughed. My boss was often amused by my irritation.

I stood in the middle of the room he'd converted to our working office in his Georgian Colonial home, my eyes fastened on his hand as magic spiraled around it. The seconds of silence stretched as his gaze stayed on me. His lips lifted into a devilish grin.

Kalen sighed. "I don't understand why you are so upset. You look beautiful. Last week you were complaining about having to deal with an irritable fae, five days ago you were complaining about wading through a sewer to find a Hearth Stone, and now you have on this stunning outfit and you're complaining. Levy, I just don't know how to please you," he teased as his eyes flickered with amusement. "Did you really think I was going to let you go to the auction dressed like a deranged hipster?"

Rolling my eyes, I sighed. "So a pink button-down and blue slacks are hipster clothes?"

He looked at the pink-and-blue plaid shoes I'd left at the door, following his "no shoes on the carpet" policy, and made a face. "They have this auction twice a year. We are lucky to be among the few people who get invited to both. So, missy, you will not go there looking like a vagabond, or some hippy hipster."

"I don't think you know what the term means," I offered.

He simply dismissed me with a wave of his hand. I looked in the mirror. I liked the hair. Dark chestnut waves draped down to my shoulders. I would've preferred my typical messy ponytail, but it was an exclusive auction, so I guessed I needed to dress up a little. The eggplant-colored dress complemented my fair skin tone and hazel eyes. But if I moved the wrong way, bumped into someone, or simply bent down too far, the "girls" were definitely going to be exposed. The cut was too low. I wasn't modest by any standards, but Kalen made me seem like a prude.

He was over the top in every way. His blond hair had hints of silver in it that nearly duplicated his silverish eyes. He thought it looked good, and as a fae, he had the option to change it if he didn't. It made him look a little older than late thirties, but quite regal. The slim dark suit showed off his sinewy build, and even if I wore three-inch heels, he had my five-foot-six-inch frame by about six inches. Kalen was a lot to take in, and the orange geometric-patterned tie was even more obtrusive.

"It's an auction. If I go in like this, I'm pretty sure people are going to start bidding on me," I teased. "Just change it." Ice laced my voice to drive in my point. We had already wasted nearly twenty minutes on this.

"You may be the most stubborn woman I know," he said with a scowl.

I shrugged and grinned. "Three years ago you gave me a job because you liked my tenacity. Now I'm stubborn? Pick a team."

It wasn't necessarily tenacity that got me the job—more like a coincidence. Our neighbor, a witch who worked out of her home, was dealing with a disgruntled fae who was convinced she was holding out on him and had a way to remove the iron ring he had to wear as punishment by the Fae Council. He'd gotten off easy, but apparently he didn't think so; however, if he'd been tried by the Magic Council, his punishment would have been worse.

One of the perks of being a fae was the ability to read thoughts, along with the ability to perform cognitive manipulation, getting people to do whatever they desired. But the rules about it were just as strict as privacy laws among humans, and he'd violated one by not obtaining consent from the person he'd been manipulating. Apparently the degenerate fae liked the "olden" days, when it was acceptable to mentally violate others. It wasn't really acceptable—humans didn't know it was being done to them then because they didn't know that fae or any of the supernaturals existed. Fae were extremely dangerous because there were no safeguards on their abilities, unlike vampires, who needed eye contact to compel someone into submitting to them.

Though the Cleanse devastated the supernatural and human world, the one benefit of it was that magic was now regulated. No more enthralling people or compelling them. Vampires couldn't do it anymore, either. If they wanted to feed from someone, they were reduced to old-fashioned seduction. Which explained why I hadn't seen any ug-mo vampires—they would probably starve to death. Nor could fae change their appearance for deception; they had to pick their features and stick with them. The penalty for changing features wasn't worth it, nor was that for their spells of the mind. There was more leniency if manipulation was done to another supernatural, but do it to a human and your use of magic was revoked.

I was just a bystander as Kalen seemed to be handling the situation and looked like he was about to subdue the irate fae. But during the struggle, the fae managed to get the upper hand, so I poured coffee on him—nothing brave, I just opened the lid and my "quick thinking and tenacity" earned me a job. Three years later, my tenacity was getting me censured.

"Nice. That's a wonderful way to talk to your boss." Sparks flew from his fingers, flashes of blue, gray, teal, and fuchsia, and I inhaled, allowing a moment to appreciate magic. To be one with it, to allow it to drape over me. I didn't have the luxury of using magic whenever the mood hit me. But the longing was there to do so, to will it to do my bidding. As the allure of it became stronger, I forced myself to think about the Cleanse. If the threat of being put to death didn't snap me out of the desire to use magic, then that certainly would.

"Hmm. As my boss, shouldn't you want to enforce a dress code?" I joked, looking at the new dress he put me in. Same eggplant color, strapless, a little longer than the other, landing just below my knees. He stepped back, giving me a long, assessing look, flicked his fingers, and a small silver necklace was placed around my neck and a goddess bracelet around my arm.

"You do enjoy this, don't you?" I asked.

He smiled, exposing perfectly aligned white teeth that hadn't become discolored by the ridiculous amounts of coffee he drank each day. It was safe to assume they were the result of fae magic. "Anytime I can get you out of the dreadful plaid shirt and tattered jeans is a win for me."

"Fine, the next time we have to go mining for things in a

cave, I will make sure I wear heels and a fancy dress. Then maybe I can stand back and bark orders while holding a flashlight, while you do all the grunt work." Sewers, caves, and disgruntled supernaturals were rare in our job. Generally, we went to estate sales, community yard sales, and storage unit auctions and answered ads on Craigslist to find merchandise. Auctions were very rare, especially one like this. In Kalen's quest to diversify his antiques acquisitions business, we'd stumbled into finding magical objects, too. In the past year, that's where we'd made the most money. An antique sewing machine was nice, but we'd get twice as much for an earth spell book.

I picked up the large tote that I used as a purse and checked the items in it: lipstick, brush, my twins—two sai— and a small dagger. We should be safe.

Kalen shook his head. "It's an auction, a very exclusive one. I doubt weapons will be needed, just cash."

He didn't push the matter when I kept them with me. Didn't matter how exclusive it was, auctions with magical antiquities always brought out the undesirables. Except they were the ones with an obscene amount of money, and whether they were human or supernatural, I was always suspicious about their intentions regarding whatever was being auctioned. For the three years I'd worked for Kalen, we'd attended Mystic Auction every six months. The first time we were invited, I was put off by the invitation process: Nothing was exchanged; a visitor came to invite you, and you were given a number that would get you into the event. An answer was required at the time of invitation, and if you accepted and failed to show up, good luck getting invited again.

Officially we were acquisitions specialists—a fancy title for getting things. We acquired objects and resold them. Sometimes we were hired by someone to find a particular object. Usually those jobs were dangerous, but paid really well. Auctions were where we acquired most of the inventory that Kalen deemed too dangerous for the general population, which he gave over to the Magic Council. Kalen had become their golden boy, and many of our acquisitions had landed him on the news. Yeah, that's all he needed, more cameras and people fawning over him. But it worked for us. I didn't want or need the publicity. I helped acquire and quietly slinked off into the shadows, content in my role as the silent partner. This time we were trying to obtain an object for a private client.

The auctions were held at the same place each time. It was a palatial pewter-colored Neoclassical home. Large pillars decorated the entrance, and as usual we were greeted by men in tuxedos under a chandelier. Dimmed lights offered soft illumination. Expensive art hung on the walls, but I didn't have a chance to really look at it or any of the unique sculptures because we were promptly escorted to our seats. Before the auctions, servers often offered a glass of wine or two. Most of the items purchased ran in the high six figures, some as high as seven, so a glass of wine was the least they could offer. I would have settled for a five-course meal.

I grabbed a glass and looked around the large room that held just twenty guests. The most I'd ever seen was twenty-five. We were seated behind a regular, Big Hat, who was always positioned front and center and wearing a hat that reminded me of something someone would wear to the Kentucky Derby. She was definitely human—there wasn't a hint of magic to her. Like so many, she was drawn to the mystique of magic, wanting to claim some for herself. Something unique and rare that couldn't be purchased on Coven Row, a street monopolized by witches and their various businesses, ranging from them reading your aura to providing protection charms.

Although most things were authentic and unique, occasionally they weren't. We'd often tried to warn her, but after several sharp comments and cutting glares, we realized she had more money than sense. The large glasses and scarf she wore would make it difficult to identify her. Which didn't bother me because most of the things she purchased were just a step above a Magic 8 Ball in their magical ability.

Most of the faces were familiar except for the guy who sat in the back dressed in all black, including dark shades that he dropped down his aquiline nose to look at me and then quickly pushed back into position. After a few minutes, he returned to slowly looking around the room, assessing everyone. Our eyes locked, human—I thought. But there was something off-putting about him. His sharp, angular features were distracting. I didn't think he was handsome, but the scowl that overtook his features bothered me. He looked like he would rather be anywhere but here. As the auctioneer took his position in front of the room, I glanced back at the stranger again. He'd taken off his glasses, his eyes cool and as dark as the clothes he wore. He finally did something other than scowl; a faint smile brushed his lips.

"I see you're drawn to the city's very own fundamentalist," Kalen whispered, pulling my attention from the stranger in black.

"What?"

"That's Daniel. The founder of Humans First?"

That explained the scowl. He pretty much hated everyone in this room, including me because he probably considered me an empathizer. Which made his presence at the auction all the more peculiar. This was a group that was very vocal about keeping humans and supernaturals separate and had suggested many times dividing the city to accomplish it.

They weren't able to be linked to any crimes to be considered a hate group, and most didn't consider them one, but the world wasn't ready to oblige them, either. The supernaturals had been woven into the fabric of society. Naturalists and clean eaters were drawn to the earth witches and their use of nature for magic. And most people paid well to find homes near the "natch," aka the supernaturals. Preppers and nature lovers enjoyed living in Forest Township, near the shifters in an area comprised of lush forestry and campsites. And they were drawn by the hope of seeing a submission fight on any given day, a chance to be allowed to have hunting competitions with actual predators, or the right to pay to fight with a bear shifter in animal form for sport. Then there was the charm of the fae and their ethereal beauty and gifts of glamour and illusions. People were intrigued by the vampires' immortality and drawn to the night dwellers because they commanded the darkness with seduction and the promise of unequivocal pleasure. HF couldn't turn people against mages and their magic, which was stronger than the witches' and far more impressive to watch than that of any illusionist.

Humans First didn't have a lot of people willing to buy into the rhetoric even when they invoked the Cleanse as an argument. And it was a hell of an argument. After the Cleanse, the world was different. It was a spell intended to wipe out all supernaturals, which was stopped, but not before it killed so many. The weakest were the first to go, a lot of them humans who had no idea that their aunt who had heightened senses wasn't just hyperaware, but a distant descendant of a fae. Or that cousin who seemed inhumanly strong and fast could trace those little assets to a liaison with a shifter. The people with a hint of magic that most considered just enhanced abilities were often descendants of some supernatural entity. They didn't have enough magic to perform it or to be classified as a supernatural. They were killed, along with thousands of other supernaturals.

Legacy was responsible for it. The others were exempt from blame, and rightfully—they were as much victims as humans were.

Regardless of Daniel's rhetoric and motives, he was dangerous. I was sure, like us, he was there to bid on the Necro-spear, a weapon that could be used against shapeshifters, who were immune to most magic in human and animal form. If stabbed with it, a shifter was not only prevented from shifting, but while it was embedded in them they were vulnerable to magic. It was created by a Legacy and possessed their magic—*my magic*.

Anything made with our magic was dangerous. Really dangerous, because we *were* magic. The purest form of it that transcended anything that people saw now. I had no hubris or arrogance about it, because I wished it weren't the case. The magic and gifts that were afforded to various supernaturals in fractions, we possessed as a whole. Our magic could affect shapeshifters and anyone else. It was the Alpha and the Omega and all the crap in between, and when all was said and done it was what broke us. I lived my life in fear that people would find out what I was, because my form of magic could perform the Cleanse.

I sat in the auction, hoping that the Necro-spear was just a rumor and not up for sale.

This auction was like the others. Kalen waited patiently on items worth bidding on. Most people came here hoping they could acquire things that hadn't been regulated or restricted by the Magic Council, and about forty percent of it was. We passed on a painting that was supposed to bring fortune upon any house it was in, and we didn't bid on a beautiful string of love pearls that Big Hat acquired. We probably wouldn't have bid on them even if we weren't holding out for a particular item. The magic that came off those things seemed off, and from the peculiar way Kalen looked at them, I suspected he felt it as well. Not only could he sense the magic, he had an extensive knowledge of magical objects. Supernaturals had an advantage that humans didn't at these auctions, which made me wonder why they would ever consider coming alone. It was like buying a used car without a mechanic. Well, maybe worse; at least you could get a warranty on a car. Once you walked out the door here, that was it. You might have just paid six figures for a junk necklace, a paint-by-numbers painting, or a decorative rock that you could have gotten at Target a lot cheaper.

The auctioneer held up a dagger. "And this, ladies and gentlemen, is a Necro-spear. It is rumored that there are only six in the world." A collective gasp was heard throughout the room.

My heart clenched and dropped to the pit of my stomach. The magic off the Necro-spear coursed through me like a wave. Its familiarity caressed my skin, and the danger of it triggered my fight or flight responses. I swallowed several times and then sucked in a slow breath that didn't help. It was indeed a Necro-spear, one of the rare things that could prevent a shapeshifter from shifting. But that wasn't the worst part. It had our magic in it and could be used to track other Legacy. Having something that was made by someone was just as bad as having their blood. If someone was inclined to believe we still existed, this could be used to confirm or deny it. I tried to remember what Kalen had said about the client. It was for a shifter, someone from the Shapeshifter Council. That was good; they would probably want to destroy it. Worst-case scenario, they would keep the spear, and it would probably be used as a submission tool to apprehend misbehaving shifters.

I wasn't happy with anyone having it, but since shifters couldn't perform magic, it wasn't that bad. I just didn't want anyone to be able to trace this back to me and expose me as a Legacy.

The bidding started out at a low four figures and quickly increased to five-figure bids, then slowed as it inched to the high five figures. Toward the end, the only people bidding were Big Hat, the head of HF, and Kalen.

The war to obtain the Necro-spear continued, and I tried to get a feel of everyone involved. Mr. HF's jaw was clenched too tight, anger—I knew he was out. Big Hat would be out soon because she'd just spent a small fortune on what might prove to be just a simple string of pearls, or worse, costume jewelry. Five aggressive bids later, Kalen was the new owner of the Necro-spear.

Before the bidding for the next object began, Daniel slipped away with two people following behind him: one a bulky gentleman whose wealth of blond hair was a little bit too long to be contained behind his ears. His rugged beard and how uncomfortable he looked in a suit made me think he was more at home with a man bun and in a pair of jeans and a t-shirt. The beautiful woman next to him was in white from head to toe. The way she wore the white strapless dress that slinked around her thin frame and six-inch heels made me want to applaud such grace. Both Daniel and the woman in white looked back at me, casting another long gaze of curiosity in my direction.

The last item, a bowl, was given a fancy name and was said to be known to help people navigate through realms. Yeah, if the realms were between two restaurants, because the bowl was as magical as the one I ate my cereal out of this morning.

Holding the beautifully wrapped spear, I fell in step with Kalen. "How well do you know the client?" I wanted to know what they planned to do with it.

"Gareth?" he asked.

I'd forgotten his name. "Yes, Gareth."

"The better question is why don't you know Gareth?"

"Why should I know him?"

"For heavens to Nancy, he's the new commander of the Supernatural Guild! And was the head of the Shapeshifter Council before taking this position."

"Who's Nancy and what does she plan to do with heaven?" I asked, a grin curling my lips as I ignored the look of derision he slipped in my direction.

Often I tried to keep my life separated from the supernatural world. My only friend in it was Kalen, and he was my boss. Staying on top of the heads of the Shapeshifter Council was more trouble than it was worth. The Mage, Fae, and Witch Councils kept the same head for years. The Shapeshifter Council was often in a state of transition, more than the other organizations, because of dominance fights. They didn't fight to death anymore; well, not as often as they used to. But they still fought into submission, and generally the one who lost was so badly injured that he was no longer an asset and was often pressured into quitting. It was hard to maintain the respect of their peers once they had lost a fight for dominance. Their dynamics were also different than those of the other sects because they still maintained small packs.

"Was he asked to step down from his position at the Shapeshifter Council?" I asked.

"No, but people were concerned about biases and efficiency if he held both positions."

"Do you know why he wants this and what he plans to do with it?"

"If he has any sense, he should destroy it. If I were a shifter, there isn't any way I would let it exist with the potential of the wrong person getting a hold of it. But it's his now, so he can do whatever he chooses to do with it. It's on him."

I really hope he destroys it. I really wished it were going to the Shapeshifter Council instead of the Supernatural Guild, which policed the supernaturals. Unlike the Shifter Council, the SG had a team of strong mages and witches on the team who, if they ever decided to believe the claims of the Trackers, could use the Necro-spear to find me and other Legacy. I doubt the leader of the Shifter Council had the same reach and access to the level of magic needed to perform such spells.

Preoccupied with my thoughts, I heard the steps—lithe, but urgent—seconds after Kalen did. I handed the Necro-spear to him and slipped my hand in my purse and wrapped it firmly around the base of the twins, letting the purse slide to the ground.

"Put it in the car," I told Kalen and turned just in time to confront the two approaching vampires. Lips were drawn back and fangs exposed, ready to attack. Vampires couldn't fly, but with the speed and grace they descended upon us, it seemed as though they had soared into position with the help of wings. They were inhumanly fast. I thrust the end of the sai into the nose of one just inches from me. Blood spurted but it didn't deter him. Vamps were immortal, but a broken nose hurt them just like it hurt anyone else; they just healed faster. He lunged again, and one of the twins pierced him in his stomach, enough to make him retreat back—but he didn't. His eyes were as empty and black as an abyss. Lifeless, but not in the typical vampy way. The lights were on but he was definitely not there. Yanking himself off the blade, he scuttled back, and when he took flight again, it was over my head toward Kalen. Grabbing the tail of his shirt, I jerked him back. He wasn't the pilot of his actions; I couldn't kill him. I shoved one of the twins into him, securing him against the ground while I took care of his partner, who was twice his width. Thick muscles coiled around his body like armor. He wasn't going to go down as easily. Times like this I wished I could use my magic, subdue him with a wave of my hand. But I might win the fight and lose in the end.

Despite his size he moved with the same lissome grace that all vampires possessed. When he charged at me, I wished I had a sword rather than a single sai. It was better to fight vamps from a distance, because once they had fangs sunk in, it was nearly impossible to get them off. I waited for him to get close enough. My shorter height gave me an advantage. I was able to use his body as leverage to climb over him. I was quick enough to dodge him, deliver a powerful side kick into his back, push him off balance, and drive the sai into him. They were both pinned to the ground, the sai embedded in them.

I had retrieved them by the time four uniformed men showed up. If you could call a black t-shirt and dark jeans a uniform. Since they all had them on, I assumed it was. The badges on their hips were enough to cause anyone watching the spectacle to part and let them through. They were Supernatural Guild officers. If you were a misbehaving supernatural, they were the last people you wanted to see. Because the officers were shifters, they were the last people I wanted to see, too. Being around a shifter was never a good idea for me. Moments later the vampires were facedown, cuffed, with two crossbows aimed at them.

I started back toward the car. Supernaturals could sense other supernaturals, but I didn't have to worry about most of them. My magic was disguised well; my mother made sure of that. But shifters, with their heightened senses, were more sensitive to it. Some said that they could smell it, and I didn't doubt it. Since the Cleanse, only the strongest of them existed. We weren't dealing with inferior shifters.

"I need a statement," said one of the guys. I cursed several times under my breath and got into the car and snatched up the Necro-spear. If they sensed magic, they would assume it was coming off it, or Kalen, so the odds were now in my favor.

"They attacked," I said when they were a couple of feet away. Caution had become a constant companion of mine.

"Without cause?" the tallest one inquired. His cool, smoke gray eyes narrowed on me.

"No, he had plenty of cause. I think he wanted this," I said, holding up the spear. The broadest shifter didn't seem to know what it was, but Mr. Gray Eyes did.

"Is there a reason you want that?"

Well, it's pointy and can kill shifters. A good weapon to have, don't you think? But I didn't say that. Instead I said, "We're meeting with Gareth to give it to him. It will be placed under his protection."

"I can take it off your hands and ensure that he will get it," he offered.

"Well, unless you also have a check to accompany that offer, I would rather give it to him myself," Kalen said. I had no intention of being present for the handoff; Kalen being there was just as good.

Gray Eyes's lips pulled into a straight line. "I can assure you the Felidae Clan can match whatever the Guild is offering."

Great, I just stepped into a nice pissing contest. The clans got along, somewhat—well, for appearances' sake. If they ever seemed to be at odds with one another, the humans started to get a little gun-and-military twitchy, ready to step in and prevent a war before it could really start. There were only three shifter clans, which made things easy—Felidae, Canidae, and Ursidae, the latter serving as the catchall for shifters who didn't belong in the Felidae or Canidae group.

The officer split his attention between me and the hand-cuffed vamps on the ground. They were still out, in a catatonic state. That wasn't typical, and I couldn't help but think about the wide, possessed eyes. Movements that seemed foreign to them and controlled by someone else, which made things even more peculiar. The only people who could master the mind of a vampire besides their sire were necromancers. We were more likely to find the Loch Ness Monster than a necromancer. There hadn't been one in years —they really were extinct. Or perhaps they existed and were in hiding. But there wasn't a reason for them not to exist; as long as they didn't control vampires, they would be fine and could speak to the dead, but not create revenants. Which I found ironic, because wasn't that what a vampire was—a revenant?

Their annihilation was their own doing, or so the stories of it would have you believe. It was in a battle, before there was the apparent civility between the supernaturals. The necromancers had set out to control the vampires and make them servants. But even the most skilled necromancer couldn't control a large number of them. The vampires chose to take the matter into their own hands and kill off the necromancers. Apparently they were successful at it, but lived with the reputation of being savages to most of the supernatural world, causing a strain.

I looked over at the vampires. I still had a nagging feeling that something seemed off. Who really was the target? Kalen? Me? The Necro-spear? The only person who seemed to want the spear more than we did was Daniel, and he wouldn't be able to control vampires in order to get it. A second thought crept into my mind and was hard to dismiss. Was this another attempt by a Tracker? Plain-sight attack and blame it on vampire bloodlust?

The SG officer couldn't take his eyes off the Necro-spear to continue questioning me.

"Do you need anything else?" I asked, stepping back, ready to return to the car.

"Your name?" he asked.

I considered giving him a fake name, but why? There wasn't a name faker than the one that I went by. "Levy ... Olivia Michaels."

"Please make yourself available for further questioning," he said firmly before he took another look at the spear and turned to walk away.

I agreed but really hoped that they could get what they needed from the gawking observers who had gathered around. As I ducked into the car, I couldn't stop thinking about the vampires and their vacant eyes and wondering who was controlling them and why.

The silence between Kalen and me was a little uncomfortable. I was dangerous with the twins, and no matter how many times he'd seen me fight, he still seemed to find something off-putting about it. I felt that way sometimes, too. My parents trained me to survive, to protect myself. My mother was an expert with the sai. The sword was my dad's weapon of choice, but at age five, when they first started teaching me to fight, I handled the sai better and never made the transition to a sword. I'd learned to use one and could wield it with a level of skill, but if I was ever up against a truly skilled swordsman, I wasn't confident I would win. With my sai, I was always confident.

A look of admiration and sorrow always marked Kalen's

face when he saw me fight. He once made the comment that behind every good fighter was a tragic past. I can't say that I agreed with him, but in my case it was true.

The buildings moved by slowly because Kalen was creeping down the streets, most of his focus on me. "Did you notice it?"

"Yeah." I sighed my response. Vampires controlled by an external force were enough to make anyone a little leery. Shifters had won the supernatural lottery: they were immune to magic. Period. And the only trade-off was they turned into animals at a full moon. Vampires came in a close second. They weren't immune, but you had to be a force to reckon with to use it against them. A simple spell wasn't going to do it. Witches and fae didn't stand a chance, and only upper-level mages could do anything to them. But controlling a vampire was a different level of magic—strong magic. Necromancer magic.

My mood mirrored his: uncomfortable apprehension. "What are you think—"

"Necromancer," he blurted before I could get the question out fully. "Would it be hard to believe?"

"Possibly." Which only brought up another set of problems. I hated to sort people into a group of "good" or "bad," but I didn't have a problem relegating them to the "creepy as fuck" category. Necromancers were now celebrated in folklore. Creative stories of their "death touch" and power to smite their enemies with something like a wisp of their breath against a cheek. I couldn't count the number of auctions that had stones and artifacts supposedly cursed by a necromancer. Yep, everyone wanted to destroy their enemy with an enchanted stone. Which was BS on hyperdrive. They had control over the dead and could perform dark magic, but to my knowledge, they didn't possess the touch of death.

But *I* couldn't destroy the world with a blink of my eye, and that's a story that I'd heard about my kind. A Legacy—it sounded so regal, and at some point we were considered supernatural royalty until our fall. It was an unfortunate saying, but it held true: we bear the sins of our fathers. But I bore the sins of a group of people I didn't know, had never met, and would probably hate as much as others did. I would forever live in fear, eternally linked to them and their sin because I possessed the same magic. I'd always be associated with a group of people who felt that they were the only ones worthy of magic and thought it was a good idea to cast a spell to kill all others who weren't Legacy. Nearly twenty-five years later, after the humans and other supernaturals formed an alliance and gave Legacy a well-deserved smack-down, I still had to hide. As far as the world knew, they all were killed. In reality, some lived, including my parents, who had me nearly five years afterward.

For years we lived normal lives, secret, existing as the odd human family next door until we were found out. My dad was killed first, giving us time to escape, but it wasn't long before my mother was found. Three years in foster homes made my parents' death even harder to deal with. Now, at twenty-three, I felt like I had paid my dues and should be forgiven. I just didn't know how to do it.

Necro-spear in hand, Kalen started up the stairs leading to the house, but I stopped to peek around to the door next to us to see if the shop was still open.

The neighborhood had been zoned for both business and residential use. Kalen used most of the home as his living quarters, but two rooms had been converted to offices. To our right were a bookstore and café. To our left was Molly's, and she was often busy. She was a witch who specialized in *effugium*, or escape. For an hour of her time, with the use of magic, she could take you anywhere you wanted to go—in your mind. Want to enjoy the thrill of the African savanna? She'd take you there. The thrill of driving in the Grand Prix? Absolutely no need to travel to Monaco. She was good at her job, but most of all, she was a very knowledgeable witch and historian. Kalen used her occasionally, but didn't require her expertise often.

His extensive knowledge had earned him the loving title of KUI, King of Useless Information. It wasn't a particularly nice nickname, but I wasn't feeling particularly nice the day I gave it to him, when he decided to keep my latte away from me until I listened to the history of the coffee press. Twenty minutes of information didn't really make me appreciate my coffee any more. Although he was a wealth of useful information, he had plenty whose usefulness I was on the fence about.

Molly's door was shut, and the closed sign was hung out. So much for my hopes of finding a convenient source for more information about necromancers. I rushed up the stairs into the house behind Kalen.

As I passed the mirror, I took a look at myself and frowned. Dirty, covered in vampire blood, with parts of my dress torn, I needed a shower and clean clothes. "What time are you meeting Gareth?" I asked.

He glanced at his phone and made a face as he looked at the condition of his own clothes. "I have to call him to confirm that I have it. He's aware that this might not have happened. This is one of the few times that a rumor actually turned out to be true."

"Give me a head start. I need to shower, and I'll be out of here in fifteen minutes." Taking a shower was my personal preference because I didn't want to make the passengers on the bus uncomfortable. Days like this, I really hated my temperamental car. It had worked for a whole three weeks without giving out on me, so probably it needed a break. I could afford a newer car, but was always reluctant to spend unnecessary money. I made decent money, but not enough to afford a brand-new car without dipping into the savings I maintained in case I ever needed to disappear in a hurry.

"Levy, you don't have to take the bus. I have a car you can borrow."

Kalen came from money—a lot of it. And although he attempted to live without relying on it, it was apparent that he could afford the costliest of accidents. He didn't think much of loaning someone a car that cost more than what they made in a year. And for a moment I considered it. I hated public transportation. But even if I didn't have time to shower and still clear out of Kalen's before the Guild leader arrived, I could get on the bus with the blood and grime still fresh from my fight with the vampires and still not be the dirtiest person on the bus. I decided not to accept the offer.

"What's your issue with shifters, anyway?" he asked, walking to the kitchen to wash his hands.

"I don't have an issue. I just think they're odd. Their extraordinary senses and immunity to magic don't bother you?"

He shrugged. "My magic wouldn't help me much against them anyway." Fae didn't possess a great deal of defensive magic, but illusions, glamours, and manipulation of mind and emotions still made them a force to contend with, except with shifters.

Examining the spear, he ran his fingers along the edges of the blade and then against the steel. "It looks like a regular dagger. I can't believe it can do so much damage to shapeshifters." It took a moment for him to pull his eyes away from it. The large blade could not only kill one, but also prevent them from shifting, similar to what one of my sai could do if it stayed embedded in the shifter. It was a hell of a weapon. But then again, my people didn't half-ass on anything. The magic radiated off it like a current. I knew Kalen felt it. He held it, studying it with interest, drawn to it more than anything we had acquired over the years. For a brief moment I wondered if Gareth would even get the spear.

"When are you going to call him?" I asked.

The question seemed to have pulled him out of the reverie state that the Necro-spear had placed him in. I was curious about what drew him to it and was about to ask when his phone rang. He answered it, and less than a minute later he said, "That was Gareth. He'll be here in an hour."

I quickly made my way up the stairs to the guest room where I always kept a change of clothing for times like this. It was better than anything in my apartment and reminded me of a posh bed-and-breakfast. The monochromatic room in various hues of blue still looked spacious despite the king-size bed in the middle of it. The closet was larger than my bedroom.

The shower hadn't taken long, maybe fifteen minutes, so I was extremely surprised to hear a male's deep voice as I descended the stairs. Gareth. Or I assumed it was Gareth. A man, at least three inches taller than Kalen, had his back to me. All I could see was his dark shirt that clung to the muscles of his back. Spear in his hand, he was engaged in a conversation with Kalen—ugh, sports. I made my way down the stairs to make a quiet exit out the back door.

"Olivia Michaels," said a velvet baritone voice. For a few seconds I considered pretending I hadn't heard him, but the deep, commanding voice was hard to ignore and I was sure he was aware of that. When he turned around, so was his appearance. Dark hair, rugged good looks, and razor-sharp features were far more impressive than his build. Full, supple lips wouldn't commit to the smile he attempted. His eyes were haunting yet alluring with a blue so light that it looked like the sky after a storm had cleared. Eyes you could get lost in, but knew could turn on you in a moment. He held my gaze for longer than I wished or expected. I couldn't decide which left me more intrigued: him, the deep indigo shifter ring around the pupils of his eyes that held the sly look of the predator that lurked behind them, or his intensity. Everything about him was a reminder of why I needed to steer clear of shifters.

"Do you mind telling me what happened earlier?"

Yep, I do mind since I just told someone from your office the same story you want me to tell you. Instead I said, "I think I told everything there is to tell to the SG officer."

The lips beveled into a frown. "I am aware of that, but I would like to hear the story from you. Based on what was told by the officer and the witnesses, you possess skills that you shouldn't, especially being a …" He stopped, slowly assessing me. "Witch?" he offered.

"No, I'm not a witch. Just your run-of-the-mill human." I gave him a coy smile. I hoped it was coy—I didn't do coy and rarely pulled it off. Based on the look he gave me, I hadn't succeeded then, either.

"Of course, that is what I suspected, which makes this even odder. How did a human woman—one probably not old enough to legally drink—subdue two vampires?"

I forgot. Most shifters have a tendency to be of the "smug asshole" variety. It didn't take long after being around them to be reminded of it.

"Well, Gareth." I kept the smile, but said his name through clenched teeth. "I am old enough, and after this meeting I'm pretty sure I am going to have a couple of shots."

"Tell me, how did you subdue two vampires—"

"I didn't do it alone, Kalen helped." His gaze briefly moved to Kalen before turning to me with the same whetted curiosity that seemed to be increasing with each second. I could see Kalen's wide-eyed look at my creative retelling of the incident. I didn't like lying and wasn't particularly happy about not taking full credit for taking the vampires down, but Gareth made me nervous. I didn't want to add fuel to the flames of his curiosity. "Did your officers tell you that they might have been controlled by someone else? Their eyes were a little odd. The lights were on, but definitely no one was home." I redirected his attention to another topic.

He nodded once. "Yes, that has been confirmed. Both of them are no longer available for questioning," he said.

"Dead?"

He nodded. "Killed themselves before they could be questioned. They were definitely being controlled by someone else, because vampires consider their existence too precious to take their own lives." He studied me in silence, stepping closer. His nostrils flared as he breathed in my scent.

I took a step back, increasing the distance between us, which he quickly narrowed as he took a step forward.

Gripping the bag of clothes I had on earlier tighter, I looked over at Kalen, who seemed to be treating our back-and-forth like a game of tennis. I shot him a look: *Get rid of him.* But he didn't seem to get the hint and instead looked expectantly for me to return the ball to Gareth's side of the court.

"Do you think it too far out of the realm of possibilities to believe it was a necromancer?" I asked, hoping to give him something else to focus on other than me, which was getting a great deal of his attention.

"Why do you ask that?"

"Most people believe they are extinct."

He smiled. "I don't usually believe in rumors of extinction, and I'm pretty sure you're not one to do it, either." His eyes narrowed as he continued to assess me with a melding of curiosity and intense interest. "Am I correct?"

"I tend to think things are extinct, but if you find a dinosaur, be sure to let me know." I tried to use that as my exit, but he stepped to the side, his tall, broad body blocking me. Cool pale eyes stayed rooted on me.

He chuckled. "I met a nymph last year. Two years ago a pixie decided to take up residence in a friend's home. A month ago we were called out because two trolls were having a disagreement. A couple nights ago, I encountered a succubus. All of them have been said to be extinct or just folklore. Nothing is out of the realm of possibility to me."

That made things even worse. *I* was supposed to be extinct. His brow rose as I inhaled a ragged breath.

I simply nodded. It was time for me to leave. I slowly started to back off, preparing to walk away. "I wish I had more to offer you. They were going after the Necro-spear, I stopped them—that's all I have. I think you should look for whoever else wanted it. I'm pretty sure that list is quite long, but Kalen can tell you who tried to outbid him."

The moment he broke contact with me to look in Kalen's direction, I trotted out the door before he could ask another question. This time when he called my name I ignored it.

CHAPTER 3

O f course when I walked through the door I was met with a view of my roommate's butt hiked in the air as she assumed the downward dog position. If she could, she would spend the day doing yoga and nights in Pilates classes. But as far as roommates go, I'd lucked out with her. Except for an occasional flash of her ass during a yoga position and her awful insistence that a superfood accompany each of our meals, she was as good as they come.

"Levy, you're all clean," she said, coming to stand and grabbing a towel off the arm of the sofa.

"I told you I had an auction to go to."

"With you, I never know. A simple pickup at an elderly lady's home might end up with you in a fistfight with a drunk fae."

I grabbed my bag of clothes and tossed it at her. She looked in it and shook her head.

"I took a shower at the office," I said as I made my way to the kitchen. My stomach had been rumbling since I got on the bus.

"I made dinner." She wiped the sweat from her face as she

followed me to the kitchen. *Oh great, now she'll see me throw out her low calorie/high energy cow-grazing food.* I was a meat-and-potatoes type of woman, and when I ate a salad I spent most of my time fishing for the bacon or chicken in it. Occasionally a tomato or cucumber would get in the way and I'd eat it. I pulled out leftovers from yesterday: chicken and rice. When she scowled, I went ahead and took out the salad she'd made as well.

"I need to eat, not graze. I had to fight off two vampires today."

"Really? What happened?"

I went over the details, and gave her the edited version. I didn't tell her about them possibly being piloted by someone else. Since supernaturals came out of the closet, humans had always been apprehensive, and who could blame them? Magic in any form could be dangerous, and it wasn't rooted in anything concrete. Why do shapeshifters change? Don't know, they just do. Why can fae compel you to truth and mages can't? It's all magic, right? Wish I had an answer. Why do supernaturals die when their magic is taken from them? Good question, that's a question that most supernaturals want an answer for, too. It was one of the downsides of being a supernatural being. Magic was as essential to their existence as their heart and oxygen. It was entwined in their essence, and their life ended the moment it was taken. Which was another thing that set Legacy apart from other supernaturals. Our magic couldn't be stolen. Many had tried and were unsuccessful. Most supernaturals' lives were rooted in magic; we were something more complex—or maybe simple, but magic existed because of us.

Savannah always had a look that was a combination of intrigue and disgust when I discussed my job. Most of the time she was intrigued. I wished my days just consisted of sorting through boxes of junk to find antiques to sell. But it was never that easy, and my conversation with Gareth cemented that. Antiquing was how it had started, until one odd find led to a bigger payoff than anything we'd ever made. People could still come in the shop and find an antique watch, an iron skillet, a canteen from the early 1900s, or a coffee press, just for the sake of having it. But if any of them were lost objects that could be used for a spell, were enchanted, or charmed and revered by one of the supernatural sects, it was a very nice payday.

"I guess you aren't going to Crimson with me tonight?" A dour look colored her words as she resisted the frown that was threatening to form.

"Of course I am." I wasn't letting her near that vamp club by herself. Of all the people I'd known in the past, she was the most rational, and yet when it came to vampires, all that went out the door. Their appeal vanquished any of her cogent thoughts, and she was reduced to a wide-eyed vamp fangirl.

The smile she brandished stayed there even as she chomped down on her banana. She didn't have many weekends off, and when she did, hanging out at the newest vampire spot seemed to be at the top of her list.

We arrived early enough that we didn't have to wait long before getting into the club. Mesmeric music met us, and Savannah couldn't wait to start moving to the beat before we'd even gotten inside. Against my strong objection, she wore a white V-neck tank top embellished in bright silver that drew attention to the neck that was on display. Her pants clung to her body and showed off the hours of work she put into exercise and dance each week. A wealth of honey-blond hair cascaded over her shoulder in loose waves, and her light gray eyes glinted when the light hit just right. I stayed close as we entered the club, hoping she didn't stumble in the ridiculously high heels that she wore to camouflage her five-foot-three height. If it were possible she would wear heels like that every day. Her height seemed to be a source of insecurity. I didn't like the feeling of walking on stilts and settled on a pair of heels just a little over an inch.

Once we were in the middle of the club, Savannah's attention flew to the corner, where a cadre of vampires were seated. The club didn't have a VIP section, but if it were to, that would have been it. A similar circle of leather seats in the back of the club gave a panoramic view of the room. The music was loud—I could feel it vibrating against my feet. A sultry, alluring beat, and Savannah continued to move with it. Although her day job as a personal assistant paid the bills, she was a classically trained dancer. Dancing was what she loved. Sinuous sways of her hips drew the attention of several vampires in the self-titled VIP section. Their stares bounced between the two of us. We were diametrically different. My chestnut hair was pulled back into a sleek ponytail, and the only makeup I wore was mascara. A thick coat of it veiled my hazel eyes. I wasn't too keen on exposing my neck in a room full of inebriated vampires, but showing up in a turtleneck was out of the question in the middle of July in Chicago. The Midwest wasn't afflicted by the same warm weather as the West and the South, but in July I couldn't tell the difference between their weather and ours. Instead I'd settled on a pair of dark jeans and pink mock-turtleneck sleeveless top.

I had taken on the role of Savannah's guardian, so it was hard to enjoy myself even as she led me onto the dance floor. I danced, fully aware of the dark eyes of the seemingly mysti-fied ginger-headed vampire who couldn't take his eyes off of her. She was equally intrigued. Her body bumped against others as she swayed to the beat, unaware of the crowd that had overtaken the room because her focus was fixed on the ginger vampire sitting in the corner. The unique and tantalizing looks of vampires for most still overshadowed and distracted from the fact that they were soulless creatures of the damned who required blood to survive. I was very aware of it at any given moment.

"Stop staring at them. I told you what happens when you stare," I whispered in her ear.

"No, why don't you tell me for the hundredth time?" she said with a stilted grin.

"Fine, be vamp kibble. I'm sure you'll manage between working out a million hours a week and your full-time job," I teased.

We had to find a medium. I was overly cautious when it came to vampires, and she was too passive. The very reasons I was disturbed by them were the very ones that intrigued her. They were beautiful monsters.

Savannah was fixated on the group across the room, eyes planted on them, desire an unfettered ball that she didn't have control of. I pinched her. She whipped around and glared at me. "What's wrong with you!"

"Stop staring."

I knew I was being overprotective and was aware that vampires weren't allowed to compel anymore because it was against the law, but I still believed that there was a little bit of suggestive messaging in their looks. Yet most of them behaved quite well since now their maker was also held responsible for them—unlike the past, when a vampire could create as many progenies as they wanted and let them run rogue, becoming society's problem. Now they needed to be with their maker for at least a year, trained, and supervised during their transition. It kept the number created down, because no one wanted to be held responsible for their misbehaving offspring.

"Will you stop it?" I barked in her ear, but she was too far gone, entranced by what had now replaced their gift to compel—their looks. People were drawn to them, ready to offer themselves willingly. The fact that some were taken over by bloodlust and killed, which I had told Savannah numerous times, wasn't enough to break the spell that the vampires had over her.

She was enthralled in a manner that reason couldn't stop, and before I could say anything, she was navigating through the crowded club the moment Mr. Ginger waved her over. I was just inches behind her as she made her way across the room. I stood at the end of the table; she squeezed in next to him. When he shifted over to make room for both of us, I reluctantly took a seat on the other side of him.

"Have a seat, love."

My eyes flew in Savannah's direction. The accent, a deep Australian brogue. She wasn't swooning anymore—she was in full-on fangirl mode. I couldn't believe this was the same woman who tried to feed me an egg-white sandwich with gluten-free bread this morning. The day before she was in my room, label maker in hand, shoving my shoes in boxes and slapping a picture and label on them, because apparently I just wasn't organized enough. I wouldn't have an excuse for rushing out in the morning because I was late. "Everything has a place" was her mantra. And she'd organized my sparse clothing accordingly. In my closet there was a section she'd labeled "someone's getting their ass kicked," clothes that were too soiled to wear out in public and had been stitched up so many times they were barely presentable. I usually wore them on our sketchy jobs where someone *was* probably going to get their ass kicked and I had to make sure it wasn't us.

"What are you drinking tonight?" he asked, looking at our empty hands.

"Nothing, I'm the DD," I said.

"Oh nonsense, that's what Uber and cabs are for. Have a drink with us."

Ginger was such an alluring presence I had ignored the other vamps sitting with him. Not much older than us, maybe mid- to late twenties. A carefully orchestrated group —a PR machine's boy band lineup, designed to appeal to whatever your preference might be. Ginger with his wide, supple lips and dimples that peeked out when he exposed his fangs. Gentle light brown eyes with that telltale silver vampire ring and a lithe build cemented his role as the charmer of the group. Dark and Broody was just that—silent as he sat at the table with his lips in a resting line. Disheveled cocoa-colored hair matched his eyes, which held just a slight tinge of disinterest. The kind that made a less cynical person work a little harder for his attention. He was broader than Ginger, but not by much, t-shirt draped casually over the cords of defined muscles over his chest and abs. It seemed he had time to do a couple of crunches between his stints of brooding. All-American had taken on his role quite well, to the point he could have invented it. The wayward smile that managed to be welcoming and mischievous. The ash-blond hair, winged cheeks, and eyes a mass of green. I was sure he didn't have to do much to convince someone they needed to be his meal.

"I'll have just a Diet Coke," Savannah said. She was just as mesmerized and bewitched as a teenager at one of the boy band's concerts.

Ginger grinned. "You have to give me more than that," he teased.

"Cranberry and vodka," she said.

He looked in my direction and waited for my answer. "I'll

take her Coke, but make sure mine isn't diet. Can't stand the stuff."

Mr. All-American chuckled as he leaned into the table. "A woman after my own heart. If you're going to do it, then do it. Right?"

Oh no you don't, Mr. All-American. You just point that smile somewhere else.

Two drinks later the boy band was taking turns dancing with Savannah and me. I still hadn't let my guard down. The Coke had me on a caffeine high, but my inhibitions were firmly intact and so was my cynicism—where they needed to be. Making sure I was on high alert. Which was why I couldn't take my eyes off the three shifters and mage who had just walked in; an odd pairing. Mages weren't as discerning and often frequented the typical vampire spots, but shifters were a different story. They preferred to stay on their side of town and frequent their clubs, which were slowly becoming overrun by college kids who were drawn to them because their drinks were stronger. With shifters' metabolisms, it took a lot more to get them drunk, and after a drink and a half in one of their spots, you were hammered.

The female shifter had to be a cat, her movements graceful and lithe as she took up a position at the bar, surveying the area, nursing her drink. In all blue—tank, jeans, and heels that made her tower over the men next to her—she was dressed like she was ready for a night out, but the stern look on her face was all business. The man next to her was a shifter, too, but a different magic came off the other man. He wasn't a shifter, but might be half, or maybe even a quarter because he was registering on my shifter-dar.

The music pulsed through the large rooms, bodies gyrated against each other, and people barely moved around

42

the overcrowded floor. I'd gotten lost in the sea of people and found myself dancing with a dark-haired guy who was getting a little too handsy. It seemed like he considered this the prelude to foreplay and maybe a one-night stand. I tried to keep an eye on Savannah as the boy band encircled her. She was in vamp heaven. I was in overprotective make-sure-my roommate-doesn't-become-vamp-food hell.

All-American leaned into Savannah, his nose brushing against her face as he spoke to her, and she gave him a whimsical smile as though he was whispering the most beautiful sonnet. *Okay, have it your way.* She liked vamps. I had to deal with it. Eventually she was going to give in to her curiosity. Maybe one bite would cure her of her obsession. I'd had my share and wasn't in a hurry to have it happen again.

Just as I had conceded she was a vamp groupie, I wasn't going to change that, and hopefully tomorrow I wouldn't wake up to Ginger, All-American, or McBroody in our apartment, Savannah's scream ripped through the music. I turned and ran in the direction of the sound, navigating through the people who wouldn't stop dancing because they were too drunk or didn't care. *After all, what should you expect at a vamp bar? They have to feed.*

I shoved my way through the bodies and found All-American latched on to her neck, his eyes empty. His fingers were entwined in her hair as he kept her close to him. Like a feral animal he gnawed on her neck, while she screamed. Then she stopped and went limp in his arms. I slipped through a small space in the crowd and clamped my hand down on his jaw. I put enough force in it to give him pain. I needed him to release her without pulling away and injuring her further. His gaze flew in my direction, and then he released her and clamped on to my arm. Blood spilled. My hand immediately went to my back, used to the twins in their sheath. I hammered blows into the side of his head, but

43

he kept his hold. Another jab, and his bite loosened. I kept delivering blows until he finally released. Blood spurted from the bite mark and he lunged for me again, his large eyes unfocused. Before I could respond, the cat shifter had slammed him to the ground. The men who were with her moved in, trying to contain the wild vampire. The crowd closed in, and someone covered my arm with a towel, which became soaked fast. I tried to get a hold of it before they took it away, but it was replaced by a new towel and disappeared into the crowd. It was never a good idea to have your blood out there, especially for someone like me, but it was too late. The commotion made it hard to see things. I pushed my way through the mass of people gathered around Savannah, who was on the ground, holding her neck, her hand covered in blood, her mouth still open in a look of surprise. Someone handed me another towel and I pressed it to her neck. *What the hell happened?*

Vamps weren't wild. Even new vampires didn't snap like that. All-American was on the ground with his eyes closed, arms bound behind his back. Since they didn't breathe, I had no idea if he was dead or not. The female shifter from earlier stood over him. The rest of his friends started toward him, but with one look she stopped them in their tracks. Her hazel eyes were smothered out by the dark brown shifter ring. Taking slow steps back, her partners tried to assist with fanning out the crowd, but people weren't listening, too busy taking pictures with their phones and looking at the spectacle. This didn't happen often, or as far as I knew it didn't happen often. The supernatural community went through great pains to keep most incidents quiet from the outside world—the humans. As far as the humans would ever know, they were your friendly neighborhood fae, vamps, shifters, mages, and witches.

Suddenly the crowd started to separate, and through the

sea of bodies appeared Gareth. *Must be nice to have that kind of clout.* He knelt down next to Savannah and removed the towel from her neck. Frowning at the deep puncture wounds, he looked at All-American and then back at her, then placed the towel back on her neck. I was sure he'd seen that same thing I had—nothing. With his face turned toward us, the vamp's eyes were empty. Just like the vampires at the auction. Someone had taken over his mind, ridden him hard, and tossed him away like trash.

"We need to get her to the Isles," he said. I started toward Savannah to help her up, but he had lifted her and was carrying her toward the door.

If the vampire hadn't just taken a chunk out of her neck and she wasn't drifting in and out of consciousness, Gareth would have gotten an earful. She might have the worst judgment when it came to vampires, but she didn't do damsel in distress—no matter how distressed of a damsel she was at the time. Glancing around at the room of glassy-eyed, wistful women, it was very obvious that most of them would have been willing to be a victim of a vampire attack to be in Savannah's place. *Be more desperate, will you?*

I rushed out in front of them. "We're parked over here." He hesitated for a moment and looked at a black Lotus before following me to the car and putting her in the passenger seat.

Once I had her settled in, I started to feel that panic. Ignoring the throbbing in my arm, I started to drive while watching her. The towel was still secured around her neck although it was sodden with blood. This was bad—so bad. The pang of guilt, frustration, and anger was hard to ignore as I drove down the street.

The Isles wasn't far, and at the speed I was going we would

be there in less than fifteen minutes. I questioned everything. Should I have called an ambulance? Why didn't I stay with her the whole time? Did I make the injuries worse?

Guilt rode me hard by the time I pulled up, only to be trumped by surprise when Gareth stood at the entrance, waiting for me. That didn't make me feel better. He would have gotten her help faster. *Dammit.*

An unconscious Savannah was rushed away as soon as we got through the door. It was enough of a commotion as Gareth updated them on what had happened that I could sneak away. I kept my arm hidden enough not to alarm anyone. I'd driven past the Isles a thousand times and never thought I would ever have to go in. It was where the supernaturals went for medical care. They were welcome to go to any hospital, but it was a preference. It was probably the least-used hospital in the city vicinity. The shifters had their own doctors. Mages and fae usually were able to heal themselves, and vampires were nearly as indestructible as shifters. When they got hurt, it was usually bad, with injuries that most would die from. The Isles was mostly for humans suffering from supernatural injury: a spell that went wrong, a run-in with a shifter, and like now, a vampire bite. I wasn't sure how many injuries were a result of any of it because they were as good at keeping confidentiality as they were at maintaining discretion. Savannah's attack would be the talk among the people in the club, but I was curious to find out if it would end up on the news. I was pretty sure a very powerful fae would visit the club and all memories of the evening would be *accidentally* modified.

I ducked into one of the rooms, holding my phone up to signify I needed to make a private call to the nurse who kept gawking at me from the station. I shot her a dirty look. It didn't work. She was probably so used to dealing with badass supernaturals, one harsh look from me meant nothing to her.

I held my bent arm gingerly to my chest. The pain was nearly unbearable, and I needed to do a spell to fix it. There wasn't a better place than the Isles, where magic ran rampant and would mask the use of mine. I could feel it, pulsing through the hallways, the variations of the different types coating the air. This was the first time I was able to get a good look at my arm. It was an angry red, with long blood trails that led away from the puncture marks where the vampire had dragged his fangs across the skin. It was a lot worse than I thought. Vampires had the ability to close up the wound, healing and sealing when they laved over it. Which was fine when you were a willing donor. A vampire bite wasn't a typical injury and remained open for a long time. It allowed the vampire to feed as long as they liked. But if unlaved or untreated, a person could easily bleed out.

I couldn't completely heal it just in case I ran into Gareth again, but I needed it to stop hurting and at least decrease the bleeding. Inching closer to the window, into the corner, I did a small spell. The throbbing in my arm receded and the puncture marks started to close around the edges, making it difficult for me to bleed out. There was still some bruising, but that was fine. Before I could completely exit the door, I was met by Gareth.

"Levy, let me see your arm," he requested in a low, rigid voice.

"It's fine." I drew my arm closer to me. "How is Savannah?"

He stepped closer, a determined look on his face. It was obvious he wasn't used to someone telling him no. "Levy, let me see your arm." It wasn't a request this time. It was a command from a man who was accustomed to having his requests followed. But I wasn't part of the Guild; I didn't answer to him. But I knew it was in my best interest to play nice.

I was prepared to do just that. Prepared to coy it up: wide eyes, pouty lips, and put a gentle timbre in my voice. I was going to work it. I'd settled on doing it, and yet this came out: "Thanks for your concern, but I can assure you it's fine. I promise the next time I'm injured and you're around, I'll damsel it up for you. And you can play the knight in shining armor. How about that?"

The stern look and straight line of his lips remained as he crossed his arms over his chest and steadied his gaze on me. His lips flickered on a smile but then settled into a faintly amused smirk.

"Savannah will be fine. When she leaves here there shouldn't be any signs of a vampire attack," he responded in an even voice.

Although I made it a habit to stay away from shifters, it was common knowledge that shifters were domineering and controlling, and the irritation that glinted in his eyes confirmed it. *Is this a fight I have to win?* I plopped the arm out in front of me so he could see the marks. I was sure he could have done without the eye roll, but I couldn't help it.

It was surprising how gentle his touch was as he ran his fingers along the marks. Warmth pricked at my skin and I moved closer to him. A simple glide of his fingers over my arm seemed far too sensual, raw and carnal. As he studied the bite mark, I studied him, once again very aware of his strongly hewn features, supple lips, and light eyes that reminded me of blue diamonds. When they held mine, I was just vaguely aware of the predator that lurked behind them. And he was a person who could not only sense magic, but could smell it. Did my shield block it? This time I considered him for different reasons, looking for hints of whether he sensed anything.

I gently pulled my arm away.

"It's a lot better than I expected. You should still have one of the physicians look at it."

I shrugged off the suggestion. I still had a blood-sodden paper towel somewhere. I had taken enough chances.

Again, that spark of irritation flared, but he dismissed it and then glanced down at my injured arm again. "What are you hiding?"

"I don't like doctors," I admitted.

After a long moment of consideration, he said, "Okay." Then he turned and headed out the door. I waited for Savannah alone.

Nearly two hours later we entered the apartment, and Gareth was right—Savannah didn't have any marks. Even the bruising was gone. But she seemed to be a little shaken up and didn't talk much on the ride home, nor once we were in the apartment. After a few minutes of small talk and very little detail about the treatment, she excused herself to bed. I felt like crap, replaying everything in my head, trying to pinpoint what I could have done to prevent the attack from happening. Reluctantly I had to admit there wasn't anything I could have done, and yet it didn't make me feel any less guilty.

I directed my thoughts elsewhere. Who was controlling the vampires and why?

CHAPTER 4

$\mathscr{I}$ tried to follow the command of the rough voice shouting for me to get to my feet. But I couldn't move my hands because they were stuck under a body. Once I slid them from under the dead weight, I saw that my arms were red with blood. When I finally pulled myself to standing I saw another body at my feet. Strands of its long blond hair splayed over my bare feet. My head pounded when I saw another body just a few inches away. A stout male, with scalp-short hair. Strong waves of magic wafted through the air and ensorcelled everything around.

"Show me your hands," a police officer demanded, his gun trained on me as was the gun of the other officer who stood next to him. I raised them as they directed and clasped them behind my head. As they slowly approached me, I noticed the same thing that caught their eye, too—another body. A shifter. And he was dead, too. *Fuck.* Three dead bodies.

My head pounded harder, the magic stung my nose and prickled at my skin. The smell of death coated the air. My mind raced over my memories—or attempted to, but there wasn't anything. *I'm Anya Kismet, no, Olivia—Levy Michaels. I* knew my address and my parents' names and the bastard who'd killed them. I could remember the day I killed him. I remembered Kalen and Savannah. I remembered everything, until—I didn't.

"State your name," demanded the officer.

I stated my name: Olivia Michaels. I looked around, hoping my surroundings would jar my memories. Savannah had gone to the hospital. I remembered that. I looked around the area. Open space, tall trees off in the distance, a bench a few feet away, a walking trail in front of it. Those were the only things I could make out in the dark. I was in a park, but I didn't know which one. It didn't look familiar to me.

Bodies. The moonlight cast an odd glow over them. There was a hint of fae and mage magic that lingered in the air. I was only able to get a glimpse of the lifeless bodies as they took me away. A waifish woman with cherub features and coltish small frame was the one who'd been sprawled at my feet. Her eyes were open and a vacant look that was a mixture of surprise and horror was carved on her face. I doubt the police officer realized that having her magic stolen was what had killed her and not the knife wound to her neck. I couldn't exactly place which one she was, fae or mage, but I was pretty sure it was fae. The man they found next to me was twice her length and broader. He had the sturdy musculature of a shifter—probably a bear or something. With shifters it was hard to tell; sometimes you could guess by their behavior if it had a lot of similarities to their animal's, but until they shifted, there really wasn't any telling. His human form made me think he was Ursidae family, but who knew, he could be a cat. His head twisted in an odd position, the turgid cords of muscle of his thick neck protruding out. How could they believe I was the one who'd broke his neck? A contemptuous scowl marred his face.

The third body was the only one whose eyes were closed,

in a peaceful state, and I wanted to believe he'd gone quietly, but he, too, had puncture wounds, in his chest. As with the woman, his magic had been stolen. The shifter was the only one for whom I could still sense the light lingering magic.

"What day is it?" I asked the officer as he put me in the back of the patrol car.

"Saturday."

Savannah had gone to the hospital on Friday. I'd lost a day. I focused on the back of the seat, trying hard to retrieve my lost memories. We'd come back from the hospital, I remembered that. Savannah had been fine, no bruises, no marks—as good as new. And that was the last thing I could remember. Did I go to bed? Did I go out?

Everything happened in such a blur; I was still trying to grasp what was going on. My head felt heavy and the constant throbbing at my temple just made the fuzziness worse. People asked me questions and I gave them the shortest answer I could. It didn't feel real until they took my mugshot, and then reality snapped me back hard, like a punch to the chest, nearly winding me. Murder. I was being charged with murder—no, not *a* murder, but three murders.

The cuffs felt uncomfortable against my skin, but they weren't too tight—just everything felt suffocating. The large office seemed too small, and the scent of smoke and various body scents, food, and oil fanned through the air. The man who sat across from me, a little too far because he had to make room for his stomach, didn't feign any interest in the situation or me, as though he'd already decided I was guilty. Dark brown eyes levied his condemnation. But when he spoke, his voice was hollow, mild. He'd slipped into his professional mask with ease, straightening his tie, turning on the recorder, and plastering on a weak but kind smile.

"State your full name," he said.

"Olivia Michaels," I said. The fog still hadn't lifted. My vision was still blurred from the harsh light they'd shone in my face in the park. And the light on his table that he had focused on me was just as uncomfortable.

"Do you know why you are here?" Once again, he spoke in a simple, even tone.

"No," I said, and his eyes widened.

"Can you elaborate?"

"I know you found me in the park with three dead people. But I don't know how I got there." My mind was muddled and I tried desperately to retrieve the lost memories.

He leaned back in his chair and studied me for a long time. His piercing eyes bored into me, the slight lift that hinted at a smile was gone, and his lips dipped deep into a frown.

"Not just *three dead bodies*," he said. He leaned into the table, his voice dropped; low and grating. "A shifter, mage, and fae. I don't think I need to tell you how bad this is." He washed his hands over his face, but the frown remained. I think the frustration had more to do with the potential media circus and paperwork that would ensue.

I closed my eyes, fighting for the lost memories to find something familiar when the last thing I could remember was Savannah going to the hospital. I told him about the incident at Crimson, an edited version. The officer didn't seem too concerned about the club incident, but still asked several follow-up questions: Was she okay? Did I know the vampires before that night? Who helped stop it?

I answered them all with as much detail as I could scrape from my fragmented memories.

His lips twisted into a moue and then he looked down at

his papers. "This is a standard question that we must ask when supernaturals are involved: do you possess magic in any form?"

Lying to people was why I was still alive, but I hated doing it. I felt like a part of me was removed each time I had to deny who I was.

"No." It was easier each time, but I hated it because being a good liar was the hallmark of a sociopath. In my case it was a quality of a survivor.

"Did you know the victims?"

I shook my head. His lips pressed into a thin line and I wondered what he was thinking as he looked at me in a ratty blue tank top stained with dried blood. There weren't any noticeable stains on the black yoga pants but I could feel the crusted patches each time I moved my leg.

His face relaxed as he blew out a breath, and for the first time his features presented something that they hadn't since the interview began. Doubt. He might not have considered me a murderer anymore, but I doubted he would vouch for my innocence, either.

Brought to a cell, I took a moment before I finally sat on the cot in the small confined space and waited for my fate. I was charged with murder; I'd be surprised if I'd be let out on bail. And I was sure my face was plastered on the news along with tons of speculation. I wondered what catchy name they gave me to pull in an audience. I looked around the cell, a human cell. The one I hoped I remained in. This was a heinous crime against supernaturals. Would I stay here or be transferred to the Haven, where they kept the supernaturals and occasionally humans who committed crimes against the supernatural community so egregious that the humans allowed them to be tried by the Magic Council? My heart started to pound in my chest at the thought of it. If things got too bad here, I could use magic to escape. But if I got anywhere near the Haven, that would be impossible. Used for people with magic, their cells were probably marked with runes and warded to weaken magic or render it ineffective, and I would have to contend with others who wielded magic and might be more experienced.

It had been a little over five hours and I'd imagined a number of ways to escape, but they all utilized some form of magic. Some required me to use strong magic. My fingers were going numb from clenching the bars. The officer who had questioned me earlier came by, a resigned look that everything was well out of his control on his face. The only thing he knew was that the Magic Council had petitioned for my release into their custody, but the only thing preventing it was opposition from two people. I had no clue who they were. Kalen? His connection to some of the members of the Magic Council because of his work for them in the past might have afforded him some consideration. But how much sway could he have in this situation?

I guessed my situation was complicated. If I were proven to have magic or be a supernatural, then there wouldn't be a debate, I'd automatically go to the Magic Council. But when a human killed a supernatural, then the Magic Council petitioned for that human to be tried in their courts. They believed that there were still biases against them and that the person would never be convicted of any crimes against them in the human justice system.

By the sixth hour, I had considered and quickly dismissed the idea of escaping. If I did, people would know and things would be worse. I would be known as a magic wielder and my hand in the deaths would seem possible. Or even worse, they would identify what I was. I would be a fugitive and would have more than just Trackers after me. I couldn't go to Kalen because I would be risking his life; they would assume he knew and had been harboring me all these years. I couldn't go home because the same would be true with Savannah. The only way this wouldn't erupt in hellfire was if I were found innocent. I was innocent. *I think.*

The Magic Council didn't have to adhere to the same rules, and they didn't. I had a better chance at a trial in the human courts' flawed system and the biases that might happen with a jury. That wouldn't happen with the Magical Court. There wouldn't be a juror who thought I reminded them of their sister or cousin's auntie's next-door neighbor and therefore couldn't be guilty of the crime. My fate would be determined by the five members of the Council. I would be my own defense, and their ability to detect lies and the use of magic made it hard to get away with much.

The waiting was getting to me; all I could think about was the rumors of how humans were treated. Supernaturals had the option of the *trials*, which they considered a lenient punishment. If you survived it, then your sentence was discharged. I wasn't sure what it entailed, but humans weren't ever given that choice because it was equivalent to a death sentence. The agreement was that humans wouldn't get a death sentence, but from the rumors, most people would have preferred it. The city usually fought hard to keep humans in their court, but I was being accused of three supernatural deaths and doubted I would get that option.

CHAPTER 5

I lay back on the cot. Twenty-three years I'd managed to hide, and this was how things were going to end—convicted of murders in the supernatural world on a day I couldn't remember. I looked at the clock. They'd made a decision in less than eight hours. That had to be a record. Usually these decisions took days. Once charges were brought, they were debated for a month, and now a decision was made in less than half a day. Did they even meet or did they just toss a freaking coin and text their decision?

I closed my eyes, listening to footsteps get closer and wondering if my decision to let myself be sent to the Haven and stand trial rather than escaping was a foolish one. At this point I'd missed my chance anyway. Whoever they would send to retrieve me would have access to magic.

Moments later, three people stood in front of my cell. *How ironic, they sent a mage, fae, and shifter to retrieve me.*

I recognized the shifter as one of the officers from the SG who took the vamps away after the attack at the auction. Up close, I had a better view of the dark gold shifter ring that coiled around his hazel pupils. He walked in front, next to the guard, while the mage and fae stood behind, dressed in dark brown suits. At least the shifter attempted a smile, but it was faint. A plaintive one, the one you give when you see a person in trouble and there isn't a thing that can be done.

The mage and fae remained expressionless when the guard attempted to put cuffs on me. The shifter stopped him. My new guards were strong: magic rolled off them and wrapped around the air, smothering the area with the power they possessed. It wasn't that they trusted me—they were confident that they could stop me if I tried anything. The mage gave me a look as though he dared me to.

For me to be a dangerous murderess accused of taking the life of a shifter, fae, and mage, Mr. Fae was standing awfully close. His thin lips twisted as his jasper-shaded gaze assessed me. Thick, long lashes made it hard to read his eyes when he cast a look in my direction. He was in desperate need of sun, or at the very least a trip to the tanning bed, and flaxen-colored hair wasn't doing him any favors.

Once we exited the building, the fae held up thick arm and leg shackles adorned with sigils.

"Do you think we need that?" the shifter asked, with a downcasting of his eyes in my direction. It was very apparent he was unimpressed with what he saw.

Both the fae and the mage stepped closer, slowly assessing me, frowns becoming deeper with each moment. They dismissed me simultaneously. I wasn't sure what I expected—a police car, armored vehicle, typical unmarked sedan—but when I was directed to a black Suburban, I didn't have the same feeling of desperate desolation as I sat back into the soft seat next to the shifter. He hadn't looked at me since they decided not to restrict my legs, and each of the others' expressions were indecipherable and professionally stoic. I had no idea if they had even made a judgment. As far as they knew, I was human, and didn't have the ability to remove a person's magic. In fact, not many people did. It required not only a great amount of power, but incredible skill as well. The silence continued as we drove out of the city to the Haven.

The city passed before my eyes and everything became so distant despite being close. Frequently visited cafés, restaurants, and stores made my heart heavy. It wasn't like I wouldn't find other friends and a place to work wherever I ended up, but this was now my home. After my mother died, I'd lived in a number of foster homes, and at eighteen this was where I settled, just outside of Chicago. An ache reached all the way to my fingertips and I took a deep breath, because I knew it wasn't an ache, it was magic urging to be released. My body was reacting to the high-stress situation, and all I needed to do was unleash it and give in to the instincts to perform magic and protect myself. But then what?

The closer we got to the Haven, the more I questioned my decision to stand trial rather than try to escape. About twenty miles from the city and minutes from the Haven, I was beyond nervous, ignoring the glaring looks as I fidgeted in the seat. The SUV took a turn, buildings became sparse, and we passed an occasional vacant one. Another turn and we were driving down a two-lane road in a desolate area. The SUV was the only car on the road, and the only things present for blocks were open fields. Finally, we turned onto a path, a building set far back, well-maintained bushes wrapped around it. A bed of fully blossomed exotic flowers extended along the path leading to the large white building and curled around the sides of it. Thorns protruded from them, and I was sure they were magically enhanced and poisonous. It didn't look like a jail at all but that was exactly what it was. A prison. The Haven. Who did they think they were fooling?

If it weren't for the rune-covered steel gate at the entrance, it could have easily passed as a business in the city. We drove around the building to the back, and the aching progressed to a throbbing. I folded the magic that was threatening to be released into me.

Just ten feet from the building my heart started to race. I could strike now and escape. The debate went on in my head over and over, but I wanted to see what the Council decided. If they found me innocent, then I could walk away, return to my life and friends and find the son of a bitch who did this to me. The doubt poked at me, the fear I denied weighed heavy as I considered the other consequences. What if they could see past the shield that masked my magic? It worked for years for me and my parents. No one could feel my magic, and as long as they didn't see the mark on me, they didn't know I was hiding any.

But what if they found the mark? Adrenaline, fear, and magic didn't mix well and it was all coursing through me, making me anxious and jumpy. When the shifter took my arm I almost slammed my elbow into his face. I jerked my arm back to my side, but he'd sensed it. His eyes became small slits and he drew back his lips, baring his teeth, his voice stern but gentle. "You *definitely* don't want to do that."

It wasn't a threat of danger from him, and I followed his gaze. The mage's hand glowed with magic that he was ready to subdue me with. The fae's eyes lowered and the sparks of anger that flashed in them pretty much guaranteed he was ready to deliver an unspeakable amount of pain.

The Haven wasn't like the jail I'd just left, nor was it like any I'd seen on television. A small room that reminded me of a dorm, with a small enclosed door to the left where I assumed they passed food. The shower was a step up from the jail cell I'd been in. After I'd showered and dressed in the black jumpsuit they provided, I was starting to feel fatigue from the lack of sleep. I lay on the bed, another improvement. It was actually soft, and the pillows seemed to have something fluffy in them instead of an assortment of rocks. Sleep didn't come, because each time I closed my eyes, I didn't see anything—nothing. A whole section of my memory wiped clean, and I wanted so badly to retrieve it and find the ass who thought I should take the fall for their crime.

Who had power to wipe a memory—my memory? A high-level mage, fae, or witch had the ability to do it, but it would have taken a great deal of magic.

Plotting revenge against the unknown assailant did make the time go by, but I wasn't sure how long it had been when two uniformed guards came and got me out of my cell, or the pretentious *stay* as they called it. They were shifters and none too gentle as they led me down the hall to what I assumed would be another room. *Great, more questions.*

Flanked by the two shifters, I worked hard to control my breathing, steady my heart rate, temper my fear. Predators, they couldn't help themselves. They were drawn to it, and based on the smile on the dark-haired shifter's face, they enjoyed it.

"Who am I going to see?"

"We'll be there in a minute."

I stopped. Tired of just following orders, I needed people to tell me something. Nothing about this situation had followed normal judicial process, and I'd realized it wouldn't once I was taken out of the human courts system. I hadn't had a phone call, not even a bail hearing. And now I was about to just *meet* with some random person. Was it a lawyer at least?

The other shifter grabbed my arm and tried to pull me forward, but I dug my heels in and snatched my arms away. When I pulled away again, he placed me in an achingly tight grip and started pulling me toward the door. He didn't see it coming, and honestly, I didn't plan it to go that way, but I yanked my arm out of his bruising grip, gave a quick front kick, and with the help of my foot caught him square in the jaw. A left jab sent him back even farther. The other shifter swiped my leg. I tumbled into him, bringing him down, too, as I hit the ground with a thud. A quick thrust of my elbow landed hard enough into his shoulder, but I missed my target—his throat. Before I could strike again, he moved and pinned me facedown on the floor, my wrist behind my back as he placed cuffs on me.

He was panting as he spoke against my ear. "Bad move."

He yanked me to my feet. I didn't care. I wasn't going anywhere until I was told what was going on. Going limp might have worked with some humans, but because of shifters' strength it wasn't an option. But I wasn't going to make it easy and just go slowly into the night, locked in a prison.

They dragged me to the door, and when it opened, they tensed at the appearance of a very angry Gareth. "What the hell?" he asked as he looked at my ruffled appearance, my legs under me as they roughly pulled me along. I was sure he came to the right conclusion.

"What happened?"

"She attacked us," the blond shifter said, his voice vibrating with anger as he pushed words through clenched teeth.

"But she's been peaceful the whole time. What set her off?"

"I don't know. I smell the fear," the other shifter said.

"She won't eat, either. The meal is still where it was placed."

I am standing right here, you know. "She," I said pointedly, "asked a simple question about what was going on and no one would give *her* an answer. *She* refused to go in a room without having a phone call or at least knowing who *she* was going to meet." I fastened my eyes on him, cooling my voice to make it sound more assertive.

He nodded slowly as he looked at the shifters again and then back to me. "You're meeting with me," he said. His voice was deep and rough, and I realized that it was the middle of the night. I was dragged out of bed and probably so was he. But you wouldn't have known it. His chestnut hair was slightly mussed, but it looked like it was from what he was doing at the moment, running his fingers through it.

I nodded. "I need to use the phone."

He jerked his head at the two shifters, asking them to leave, and then he opened the door wider. I didn't move, firmly rooted in the middle of the hallway, obstinacy in the driver's seat. "Phone. I need to use a phone."

"My hearing is fine, I heard you the first time. Come in," he said in a cool but mild tone.

Any gentleness that he'd possessed was belied by the stern look in his eyes. He appeared to have had the same couple of days I'd had, but I doubted he lived in a place as cramped as the *stay*.

He waited patiently for me to walk in and take a seat in the metal chair across from the large wooden table. The county jail paled in comparison to the Haven. The walls were light yellow and a layperson would have thought the designs on the walls were art, but they were spells used to inhibit magic. It was so strong that it drifted over my skin and pricked at the tiny hairs on my arm. They didn't need to put rune-decorated cuffs on me to prevent me from doing magic

—the room had enough magical wards to prevent the average magic user from performing any. If I were a typical magic user it would have stopped me, too.

Gareth moved in silence as he came behind me and unlocked the handcuffs.

Gently I rubbed the red line that had formed from their tightness. As he tossed them on the table, I asked, "I guess you don't consider me dangerous?"

His lips formed a half-grin and only displayed a hint of perfectly aligned white teeth. "I'm quite sure you are dangerous, but I don't fear it is to me. I'm not as easily subdued. But I'm sure you know that."

Arrogance and confidence were so often confused, but he seemed to possess a great deal of both. He slipped in the chair with such ease of movement I was reminded that I was dealing with a predator, a skilled and probably deadly one.

Crossing his arms, he relaxed back in the chair. "What happened in the park?"

"I would like to make my phone call first."

He repeated his question, his voice harder than before, his stormy, narrowed eyes fixed on me. "You will get your phone call, but you will answer my questions first." It was a reminder, just like my first conversation—people didn't deny him. Or at least it seemed like an expectation of his.

I closed my eyes and tried to retrieve memories that were still lost. Just a blank space where that day should have been. "The only thing I can actually remember is the night at Crimson."

He leaned in, studying me closely, his silver-blues holding mine until I dropped my gaze and looked at my hands. When I lifted my eyes they were still rooted on me. "Finish."

"I took Savannah home, and we talked for a little while and then went to bed."

"You sleep in your clothes? You were found fully dressed."

I was going to sound like a crazy person if I told him that I slept in clothes that, if needed, could pass for street clothes. It was a habit, yoga pants and t-shirt. A small bag of clothes and all the money I had saved over the years stowed away in it. At any time I was prepared to run if I were ever found out. There was a difference between a Tracker knowing of my existence and someone like Gareth, head of the Supernatural Guild. A team of skilled, trained shapeshifters, high mages, and elite fae wasn't something I could go up against and survive. I gave Gareth a once-over. Thick bundles of muscles laced up his forearms. His broad chest strained the seams of his t-shirt, and a defined core wasn't easily hidden in said t-shirt. He was muscular enough to be powerful, and lean enough to be quick. His lips curled into a miscreant smile. "What are you thinking about?"

Jerking my eyes away, I stood and began to pace the room, aware that he was watching me. "I'm just trying to remember ... but I can't. I can't give you anything else."

"Witch, low mage, or fae?" he asked.

"What?"

"Which are you? I'm having a hard time telling. Your magic smells different."

"You asked that question before, remember?"

His lips twisted into a frown, and curiosity flashed and quickly settled. "I know, but I'm rarely wrong."

"You think my answer would change between the last time you asked and now?"

He shrugged. "I'm just asking a standard question." Behind his eyes lurked something that I couldn't quite place. His curiosity was definitely piqued. "I don't think I've ever been wrong before."

I shrugged back at him. "There is always a first time for everything."

He attempted a smile, but his obvious doubt made him unable to hold it. "Perhaps."

"May I use a phone?"

He grabbed the phone and slid it across the table. I looked at it for a moment before I took it. Did I want to call from his phone and give him access to numbers I called?

He chuckled to himself. "Don't you think I can get the numbers of whomever you've called, ever?"

"I'm sure you can, but why make it easy for you?"

The grin lingered as he closed the door behind him.

Savannah was the first person I called and her voice was weighted with concern and fear when she answered the phone.

"It's so good to hear from you. When I heard that you were being transferred to the Haven—" She stopped and sighed into the phone. Distress made her voice shaky.

"I'm fine. It's like a freaking dorm here. It's not like I'm in jail." I made my tone light and lively. She would stress, but I wanted her to do it less. The *stay* wasn't that bad. But it *was* just like I was in jail, a supernatural one, but a jail nonetheless.

"What about bail?"

"I'm a suspect in a triple murder. I doubt I get bail."

"I spoke to my dad and he said you had to have a bail hearing." She sounded like she was ready to suit up for a one-person protest against the machine.

"Savannah, you can put the marker and poster board down, I'm fine. Things don't work the same in the Haven and with the supernatural laws. It's not that bad. I'm using a cell phone and when I get back to my room—and yes, I did say room—I'll have something to eat similar to what I had earlier, which was a cheeseburger and fries."

"See, that's how they get you, a slow death from coronary disease." Her light, melodious laughter was a welcomed sound. The tone of her voice relaxed, although I knew it was for my benefit. "So what happens next?"

"They can't link this to me. Those deaths were caused by something supernatural. It couldn't be me, and they will figure that out and let me go," I asserted with a calm that I didn't really feel. Then the unsettling thought came to me. *I could have done this.* I had it in me. The ability to rip the magic from someone and take their life was something I had the magical power to do—but I wouldn't.

They'd checked me for shields, something used to block the detection of magic. Few witches could do the spell, it cost like hell. But if you were trying to hide that you possessed magic, you would pay whatever it cost. My mother's best friend had been a powerful witch and made mine. I blinked back the tears, remembering that she'd died as a casualty of knowing my family and who we were.

I pushed away the memories. One thing at a time. Get out of the Haven and find whoever set me up and make them wish they had made better life choices.

"I'll be home clogging my arteries and finding a million ways to avoid going to yoga with you in no time," I teased.

I sounded confident enough to be easily believed, and she was all brightness and sunshine on the other end. We were both full of crap. But crying about it, being depressed, and thinking about the alternatives wouldn't have changed anything.

"Did I make the news?"

"No." She sounded just as surprised as I was. But then again, was I really surprised? To keep the peace and calm, supernatural crimes were handled with a level of discretion I'd never seen before. Once the supernaturals were forced out of the closet, Humans First became a small but vocal group that didn't like it. They didn't like magic, period. Living separate was one of the reasonable outcries, less radical than it was initially. They were too small to be anything more than an annoyance, but if supernaturals were considered a threat, then it would add legitimacy to their views. Most people liked the way things were, and the idea of a war between the supernaturals and humans would be devastating. The reason they'd come out the victors against the Legacy and stopped the Cleanse was because they'd worked together. The alliance benefited both.

CHAPTER 6

*A*fter the breakfast I couldn't bring myself to eat, I was led upstairs by two different guards—two mages. They must have heard about the incident the day before because they were stone-faced as they removed me from my room. And the looks didn't soften, even after I was led into the large room that took up at least a quarter of the top floor; white walls with runes that could be activated or deactivated with an invocation and sacred passages that denoted their commitment to hold up their laws, to protect the human and supernatural, and to provide punishment befitting of the crime, besides all the other things that made them feel holier-than-thou and worthy of passing judgment on others. The large dark wood chairs, with ornate carving, deep burgundy crushed-velvet cushions, and bejeweled armrests, looked more like thrones than chairs. In fact, their chamber made me feel like I was in a cathedral. Large frosted windows covered half the wall, thick muted-colored drapes pulled back to allow a distorted stream of sun in.

I stood in front of the oversized bench. They were all dressed in black suits. Constantly being surrounded by black made me feel like they were gently ushering me into an acceptance of death; sending subliminal messages to me to prepare for it, because it was mine.

Five people including Gareth watched me with intrigue and aversion: a mage, fae, witch, vampire, and shapeshifter. All sects represented. I didn't know why the vampire was there; what was so damn magical about them? *The walking dead. Big deal, they might as well have a hot zombie sitting in his place.* But he was a big deal. I didn't know him personally, but I was dealing with the strongest and most respected of each division.

The fae, Harrah, was the first to speak as I knew she would be. She was the face of the Magic Council and the only one besides Gareth that I knew by name. *Shouldn't there be some type of introduction?* I should know the names of the people who had my life in their hands. I only knew Harrah Siels because her name was always placed on the bottom of the television screen. She was the greatest PR person that the magic community could have asked for. A rogue shifter went crazy in a bar and killed a bunch of people, Harrah was on camera. Her gentle reassuring amber eyes, round cherub face, and supple bowed lips and petite stature lent to her seraphic appearance. Her dainty voice and genteel demeanor entreated trust. Magic wasn't scary, ominous, or dangerous when she was the face of it. And that seemed to be her job. Harrah was good at her job.

And always surrounded by a group of the Magic Council's representatives, who often looked as though they could handle themselves in any situation. Whether it was a spell that had to be stopped, a curse that needed to be lifted, a shifter who needed to be controlled, a mage who needed to be disarmed, or a freaking kitten that just needed help getting out of a tree, they could handle it all, and so the human world felt safe.

"Will you please tell me your full name?" Harrah asked, and I felt the warmth of her magic wrap around me, making an attempt to force me into truth. It was illegal to do this anywhere outside the court. But their court, their rules. They established the truth by all means.

Her magic was strong, but it didn't take much to put up an *apotrepein*, a magical wall, to block it. But I watched everyone's face to make sure they didn't sense it. Magic didn't work very well on my kind. It worked, but it had to be very strong. Perhaps if another fae had been there to help, then I would have actually been forced to put up one powerful enough to be detected. I gave her my truth. I was Olivia Michaels. I had been her longer than I was Anya Kismet. The moment I donned the brunette hair and got rid of the trademark fiery persimmon mane, the Legacy trademark, and had the shield tattooed on me to mask my magic, I became Olivia.

I said my name with confidence in my lie, "Olivia Michaels," and tried to keep a steady gaze on Harrah, but like everyone's in the room, it slipped in Gareth's direction. He leaned back in his chair, studying me.

My heart started to pound harder the longer he took, and his smirk didn't help. *Say something!*

"Will you repeat your name again, please." His voice was low, but his command held the necessary effect.

Was he screwing with me?

I repeated my name through clenched teeth.

He shrugged. "She's telling the truth."

The tension in the room relaxed and all eyes immediately went back to me.

My lies and restrictions had become my own personal prison. My life was slowly turning me into a deceiver, and I realized I needed to be one in order to survive, but it was getting harder.

The witch was the first to question me. "Are you able to use magic?"

I shook my head. She studied me with the same intensity as Gareth had before looking in his direction.

He nodded to signify I was telling the truth. The tight furl of her lips relaxed. More questions were asked, a repeat of the ones asked at the jail and by Gareth.

The mage questioned me next. He seemed the most comfortable in his role as judge and executioner. Sitting back in his chair, he steepled his fingers. His tailored black suit hung pleasingly over his body and complemented his slim physique. The white shirt was crisp and bright. Sharply hewn features went further than what some might describe as "chiseled." They were dagger sharp, and amber eyes homed in on me.

"It is your defense that you don't remember anything from the other night. Just waking up next to the dead bodies. Is that what you want us to believe?"

"It's not just a defense, it's the truth," I said.

Nothing could have prepared me for the jolt of pain that seized my body, bringing me to my knees. It was as though someone had taken my insides and twisted them in a heated vise. My nails bit into my skin and I fought the urge to absorb the magic and send it back at him even harder. I didn't look up, but instead kept my head bowed down, because if there was a smug look of satisfaction on his face, I would have wanted to wipe it off by any means. I panted and it took a few minutes to get my breathing under control and deal with the pain. A tinge of magic still flared in me, a gentle throb.

"Jonathan, that was unnecessary," Gareth said, keeping his eyes on me as he addressed the mage.

"I don't feel that it was. Perhaps she needed her memory

jarred a little. She now knows there are consequences if she is dishonest."

After a pause, Gareth directed his attention to Jonathan. With a hand to his chin for a while, he appraised Jonathan in silence. He was intense, his anger tightly gathered, ready to explode. If they had forgotten he was a shapeshifter by his previous somber mood, they were very aware of it now. He commanded the room. "I've interviewed her and told you I didn't think she was guilty of the crimes, and if I felt she was being dishonest, I would have told you." His gaze sharpened and fixed on the mage. He leaned in, and his tone dropped to a low growl as he spoke. "Don't do it again."

Although he was one of the two people who didn't possess magic, he was the scariest person at the table.

Jonathan sat up and looked quickly in my direction. "Ms. Michaels, go on with all that you remember."

And I did. I told them everything. They listened in silence, while Gareth and Harrah did most of the questioning. It wasn't until the questioning led to what occurred at the auction and the club that the vampire finally seemed interested.

"What makes you believe that they were being controlled by something else and not just in a state of bloodlust?"

"I've seen vampires in bloodlust," I admitted. I'd seen two, which didn't make me an expert, but you don't forget what they look like when they attack. "It's a different look, more desire, a need ... like they are ..."

"Horny?" he offered, as a lascivious look brushed over his features. I was sure he'd been told he was handsome more times than he ever needed to hear. As his fingers raked through his gilded blond hair, an odd contrast to his dark eyes, he looked at me the way most vampires looked at any moderately attractive person, as food and possibly more.

And if you didn't serve any of those purposes, they quickly lost interest.

"No. Hungry. An insatiable hunger."

He nodded slowly, and although he continued to look at me, apparently I was still on the menu. He addressed everyone else. "If my vampires are being controlled, it is by a necromancer. How is that possible?"

And that wasn't even the most pressing question. Why were necromancers risking being discovered?

The vampire addressed Gareth. "Do you believe it could be the work of a necromancer?"

Everyone looked in Gareth's direction. He considered the question for a long time and then frowned. "I don't know, but it definitely isn't something that we should rule out."

Jonathan cleared his throat, clearly agitated that the conversation had digressed, or maybe he wanted the trial to be over because he was getting a little light-headed from sitting on his high horse.

The interrogation continued for forty more minutes, and most of it consisted of the same questions being asked different ways. With each question they seemed tenser. Cold. And then they simply dismissed me in the middle of a question. Harrah said they had enough and called for someone to escort me back.

When the same shifters came into the chamber to retrieve me, I hesitated before going with them. I looked over my shoulder at the Magic Council, trying to read their expressions, and not even Gareth looked in my direction. Instead he kept his head down. Maybe they didn't think I was guilty of the murders, but they thought I was guilty of something. Panic quickly took over the darkest parts of my mind, and the fear blossomed into terror. Did they know? Could they have sensed the rise of magic in me, when Jonathan attacked, and known it was different than theirs? It wasn't mage, fae, or witch magic. It was one brand, undiluted and strong, ancient strength before magic was labeled and controlled, before it was sorted and divided. I wasn't something scary and wrong, but my magic damn sure was. I sucked in a ragged breath, and when I exhaled again, I made an attempt to control my breathing. The shifter on my right kept looking at me, and I was sure he could hear the increase in my heart and the change in my breathing.

Back in the room, I waited, pacing the floor and stopping each time I thought I heard footsteps. I had gone to the small window twice. It was big enough for me to fit through, but I thought about the beautiful vines of flowers that laced up the side of the building, which I was sure were cursed to cause great harm if someone even considered climbing near them. And there wasn't a way to climb out the window and avoid them. By the second hour of waiting, I pushed the bed toward the window to get a better look at the flowers along the wall. There was such a potent scent, just getting close to the window made me light-headed—a sedative. Plans went through my mind, and each one ended with me being on the run. I had to just wait.

Hour three, I heard footsteps, the door opened, and Gareth walked in. "You are free to go," he said.

"That's it?"

He nodded once and handed me a bag with my things in it. The clothes were washed, but not well enough to get out the blood. The black yoga pants didn't show it, but light stains remained on the t-shirt. I stepped into the bathroom and quickly dressed. He was leaning against the wall when I returned.

"I can give you a ride home," he offered.

Why didn't I accept? Who was I fooling? I knew why. I'd been lucky; he hadn't sensed the magic. But the more I was around him, the greater the chances of it being discovered. I couldn't let my guard down around him.

Kalen nearly crushed me when he hugged me. He was wiry, but stronger than most people. "How did you get in this mess?" he asked as I dropped into the seat of his Audi.

"I have no idea, but when I find out who did this to me, I'm going to rip out something they are really going to miss." But I didn't know where to start.

I didn't mind telling Kalen what had happened, but he seemed strangely intrigued by the Haven and Harrah. She was an enigma, loathed and loved. If the supernaturals had a reality-show queen, she was it. The gentle face of the supernatural world that they trotted out in front of the cameras to remind humans that magic was innocuous, although we all knew that it had a dark side that was often regulated by laws.

By the time he dropped me off, he had heard everything, including what Jonathan had done to me.

Responding to the anger in my voice, he said, "Levy, sometimes you have to let things go, including finding out what happened. Let the Guild handle this. Someone who is strong enough to wipe away your memories isn't someone you want to go after alone." He was more than urging me. It was a brotherly order.

"But why me? Aren't you curious?"

"Not enough to risk your life," he said. This wasn't just a simple urging—he was laying on the guilt trip, and "no" wasn't an option.

When he drove up to the house, I tried to get out before he coerced a promise out of me. As the car rolled to a stop, I jumped out and waved as I ran up to the door of our apartment. I didn't think about the hard look I knew he was giving my back as I searched for my keys. And when I opened the door, I waved at him again, quickly entered, and closed the door behind me. Resting my head against the door, I looked up to find Savannah sitting at the kitchen table with cupcakes. Real cupcakes—chocolate—and not the low-fat crap that was sweetened with applesauce and contained some unholy version of unsweetened fake milk that she usually tried to shove down my piehole. I could smell the sugar, chocolate, and delicious full-fat ingredients as soon as I was in reach. *Yep, delicious empty-calorie goodness that's going to take at least a ten-mile run to burn off.* But I didn't care, and although her lips wavered a little into a disapproving smile, I scarfed down one and started working on another before I took a seat.

"So everything's over, right?"

I spoke between bites. "I'm no longer a suspect in three murders. But there's still someone out there stealing magic who wanted me to take the blame for it. No, it's not over. I need to find out who is behind this and why."

Although she didn't voice her objection, her frown deepened and she pressed her lips into a thin line. Between her disapproval and Kalen's concern I was going to feel guilty pursuing this, but I had to. Something was gnawing at me about this situation. It seemed like there was more to it —much more.

We talked for hours as she questioned me about everything from what happened to the clothes that I wore while at the Haven. We continued to talk, with her rehashing stories about her job and family that I'd heard a thousand times before. She would've done anything to keep me under her watchful eye. The oldest of three children, she had protective instincts working in overdrive. As far as she was concerned, she went to sleep and I went to jail, and in her crazy mind they were somehow connected. I wasn't going back to jail or the Haven on her watch.

The questioning and talking would have gone on all day, but by the evening, I pulled out a bottle of wine. She declined until I coerced her into having a celebratory drink with me. A glass and a half later, she was in a white wine–induced slumber. I hated doing it, but I knew I would never get out of her sight, and I had work that needed to be done.

For a while the guilt ate at me as I watched my friend sprawled out on the sofa.

$\mathcal{O}$nce I was convinced Savannah was going to stay asleep, I grabbed the twins and put them in their sheath and headed out the door to investigate the crime I was charged with.

The park was empty and dark as I suspected it would be at four in the morning, but the streetlights and my flashlight provided enough illumination. I took a few steps toward the scene of the crime. Although I suspected all evidence of murder had long been cleared away, I hoped something might have been missed. I looked around the dark area; billowy trees surrounded the park, the lights cast an ambient glow over the benches, and I could hear the sound of crepuscular animals off at a distance.

I knelt down near the area where they'd found me and for a few minutes debated if I should try a reenactment spell, but quickly decided against it. I was desperate, but not desperate enough to try something so powerful out in the open. My decision was only confirmed when I heard the light steps behind me. One from my right, the other from my left. I gripped my sai, and when the intruders were within striking distance, I spun my arms and shot out the blades, just inches from their throats.

The streetlights cast an unappealing shadow over their features. They might have been soft in their movements, giving the illusion that they were professionals at this, but they weren't. People who'd had their share of brushes with death didn't blanch like they did. They were dressed in twin spy gear, dark jeans and black t-shirts that clung to their broad, defined physiques from an excessive amount of time in the gym. But it wasn't just to weight-lift—they moved with a fighter's refinement, definitely light and skillfully trained to move and disable, but I doubted they used the skill often. Poster guys for every spy movie I'd seen. Mussed hair, just enough to let you know they weren't stereotypical pretty boys. Faces stern, but not cruel. Each was ready to shift from good cop to bad cop at a moment's notice. Tall Spy Guy spoke first as he stepped back just a few inches before he moved my hand away. The shorter Spy Guy seemed too afraid to respond. I dropped the sai to my side and took several steps back, maintaining my defensive stance and ready to engage if necessary.

"You're dangerous with those," he said, smiling. Maybe I was wrong about him. Danger didn't bother him, but his shorter counterpart still looked like he was going to lose his dinner and perhaps everything he'd eaten in the past week.

"Aren't most people with sharp things?"

He smiled, so crooked and wayward that in any other situation he would have had me blushing. "Not necessarily. If you don't know what you're doing, then it's just entertaining to watch."

"I'm Clive." He extended his hand, exuding more confidence than I'd have expected from a person who was weaponless.

Clive. Of course, that's probably number five on the list of acceptable spy dude names. I stared at his hand. "I'm a member of Humans First," he said proudly.

This guy is a walking cliché.

I relaxed. There wasn't going to be any violence, just a bunch of talking and schmoozing. They would give me their spiel about the human race being special little snowflakes that needed to be protected from not only the things that went bump in the night, but those that managed to do it in the daytime, too. His face settled with interest and amber eyes displayed cautious curiosity.

"How did you do it?"

"Do what? Almost stab you with the twins?"

"Twins?" His response was laced with innuendo.

Leave it to a guy.

I lifted the sai, keeping a grip on them, and made a show of whirling them in a little circle before sheathing them at my hip.

"No, how did you kill the mage, fae, and shifter?"

I stared at him for a moment. *Is he kidding me with this?* "I'm innocent, you know."

There was a devious undercurrent to his words as he gave me a roguish smile that brightened his eyes and said, "We are all innocent until someone can prove we aren't."

I frowned at the insinuation, and my hand twitched with the need for violence. *I may have underestimated him.*

"Well, I *am* innocent," I said.

"Let's assume that you are innocent, but you've learned how to manage the supernaturals, using their powers against them. Is it something you can teach us, or do you have a magical object that can do it? I've heard the rumors of these things existing."

HF thought I was guilty and was ready to recruit me for their legion of misguided humans ready to take back their

81

city. "A magical object with the ability to remove magic from someone without the user having magic is a rumor. No such thing exists." If it did, I didn't know about it, and I really wanted to squash any hope that one did. They were the last people who needed to have access to something like that.

"And I can assure you that if anyone suspected I was guilty, I wouldn't be here having this very uncomfortable conversation with you and this guy"—I jerked my head to the nervous Spy Guy—"giving me what I assume is his menacing glare." Turning my attention to him, I said, "You should work on that. Cross your arms. Then draw the frown in a little more and suck in the cheeks. Dimples aren't menacing. Your brows are thick enough, bring them together a little. Give me a seethe, like a fire-breathing dragon. Try my little suggestions …"

Before I could finish, he had done them all. Eyes closed slightly to form little slits, breath forced through clenched teeth, muscles pulled taut around the neck. *I knew he could do it.*

"Yeah, like that," I said when his glare intensified.

I returned my attention to Clive, who seemed very amused. "Thanks, Clive, but I'm not interested. Seriously, if anyone thought I was guilty, do you really think I would be here?"

"Yes, we lobbied quite aggressively for your release. We wanted you in our court system, not theirs."

"How kind, but it didn't work," I pointed out. I really needed this conversation to end, and to let him know in no uncertain terms I wasn't interested. If they thought I was guilty, I'm sure people in the supernatural community did as well. The last thing I needed was to be seen with them. "I'm not interested, so I suggest you don't waste any more of your time, or others', contacting me again. It's a no—infinity. Does that count? So if you're hanging out at a meeting and think 'Hey, let's ask that Levy woman to join,' remember I said 'infinity' and dismiss the idea. Okay?"

I smiled, trying to temper my words, although I really just wanted to tell him to screw off and stop bugging me, but apparently—as Kalen had pointed out several times—people considered that rude.

I turned my back on purpose and started to survey the area, mostly to demonstrate my disinterest, but I also needed to see the type of person I was dealing with. I glanced over my shoulder. He was still there, and I didn't think he was going to attack, but he seemed like he wouldn't mind plunging a knife in if given the opportunity. That made him very dangerous. I took the opportunity to make sure there weren't any more HF members skulking around. Off to the right, I saw the yellow glow of animal eyes lurking from behind a large group of trees. When it caught my eyes, it receded back. *Shifter—dammit. That's not good—not good at all.*

"Whether you did it or not, there is something about you that has made HF take notice. We want you on our team."

"Well, if you guys were any good at your job, you would know I don't play well with others. I think I was quite nice with declining. Now you're just being a pushy salesman. I'm not interested. To be honest, I like the way things are, so I'm not trying to change it. And just for the record, 'Humans First' sounds like a bank. Just weird and kind of corny. You might as well have called yourself the Justice League." I grinned and playfully looked around. "Where's the archery guy?"

"That's the Avengers," short Spy Guy offered, taking a break from glaring and seething. His face flushed with irritation.

"Oh, I always get them mixed up. But one point for you,

knowing your superhero franchises. Good for you." I grinned. They stood firm without any plans of leaving.

I sighed. "Thanks, but no thanks."

Clive wasn't going away, and the other Spy Guy had perfected his glare and menacing look and was laying it on a little heavy. I started to walk away; maybe that might drill it in that I wasn't interested. I had gotten about three feet away.

"Either you are with us or against us," Clive said, his voice edged and cool. I turned, and his look had changed. The genteel mask that swathed his features had been replaced with something ominous, dark and cruel. It might have worked on someone else, but once you'd been through what I had, there weren't a lot of things that provoked fear—especially a look from a Spy Guy in a group with a goofy name.

Although his features relaxed, his crossed arms made his biceps stand out, exposing well-developed muscles and a tattoo that I couldn't quite make out.

I chuckled, light and whimsical. "When you make a threat like that, shouldn't you be stroking a cat and laughing maniacally?"

His deep, roaring laugh filled the air and his arms relaxed at his side. "I think this conversation went south fast. Accept my apologies. Think about it, and if you have any questions, call me." He approached me and handed me his card. The genteel and placid smile reemerged as quickly as it had disappeared. Clive was a situational chameleon. He was neither good cop nor bad cop, but whoever he needed to be to get the results he needed. That not only made him dangerous, it made him untrustworthy.

My smile matched his and was probably just as insincere. "Of course. Thank you."

And I walked away, scanning the area, trying to take it in as quickly as I could to pick up on anything I had missed. Except for the slight tint of blood on the grass, there wasn't anything I hadn't caught when I arrived. There wasn't anything there. Even the dense web of magic that had clung to the air the night I'd been picked up was gone. It wasn't as though I expected it to be there, but it was magic that I wasn't familiar with and hadn't been exposed to before.

CHAPTER 8

I pushed my way through the door with my shoulder, two coffees in hand. Kalen leaned against my desk, waiting impatiently for his morning fix. But before he could take his coffee, a caramel macchiato with an extra shot of espresso, from my hand, he turned his nose up at me as he gave me one disdainful sweeping look. It didn't look like we worked in the same place. Dressed in a pair of tailored slacks, he sported a sleek tan button-down rolled up at the sleeves, a couple of buttons undone. A brown jacket lay over my chair, next to a large box, I assumed an estate find. Those were the worst. People were just lazy. They would just shove in a bunch of things that they had no idea what they were and sell the box. We'd become the go-to company for it, and sometimes it was profitable, but most of the time it was us wading through a bunch of things that had little to no value.

The frown deepened and he gave me another sweeping look. Trailing over my jeans, that were fading a little, and my red-and-black plaid shirt his gaze went down to the Converse sneakers and then it shot up to the loose bun on top of my head. He rolled his eyes away, and then his finger shot up.

"If you change my outfit, the coffee goes in the trash," I hissed, hovering his fix over the can.

"Okay, miss," he said in the low, calm voice that negotiators used on television shows. "No drinks have to get hurt. Put it down on the table and step away. No one has to get hurt, no beverages have to die."

I pushed the cup toward him. He took a long drink from it. "I didn't think you would be in today."

"Why?" I asked, peeking into the box. It looked a little more interesting than most, and I was in a hurry to get through it because there was a subtle hint of magic. It couldn't be anything really powerful, because I didn't feel it until I was right on the box.

"I figured you needed some time."

I needed to work. Kalen paid me better than what I could make anywhere else, but it wasn't enough that I could afford to take time off "just because."

"No. The more time I spend idle, the more frustrated I get."

"The murders?"

I nodded. "I don't know how I got there. I can remember everything except the time between me getting in my bed the night of the vampire attack and waking up next to the dead bodies. Who has the ability to do that? And why did they pick me? Was it just random?"

His mouth twisted to the side as he looked down at his coffee. "It happened again last night, but this time it was a fae, mage, shifter, and witch."

My heart skipped. On the day I'd been released. This was bad. Really bad. It only got worse when the office phone rang.

I grabbed it, softened my voice to saccharine sweet,

shifting into receptionist mode. "Hello, Kalen's Collectibles. How may I help you?" I forced my eyes not to roll at the cutesy name.

The person started to speak, but stopped, getting out only, "Olivia Michaels?"

"Yes."

"This is Gareth; I need you to come to the Supernatural Guild office at eleven." And then he hung up.

I groaned when I looked at the clock on my phone: it was a little past nine. The Guild's office was nearly a half an hour away, and as usual my car had decided it needed another day off. Taking a cab would be expensive, and public transportation would be a pain in the butt. I considered calling him and telling him that I couldn't do it. After all, if it were in regard to the incident last night, he would have arrested me or brought me in for questioning. Right? But maybe this was him playing nice, and if I didn't come in, then it would be the equivalent of me being guilty.

Kalen took me to the large light gray multistory building that didn't look like any precinct I'd seen before. The windows were large, wide. Dark drapes were drawn back and could be easily seen from the street. Beautifully manicured shrubbery surrounded the building on a lawn that looked freshly cut and well cared for. Large oak trees swathed the walkway, and people spilled in and out of the building, some in uniforms, but most dressed in business casual. A few taking liberties with "casual" and wearing just t-shirts and jeans. I wouldn't have thought they worked there at all if it weren't for a badge dangling from around their necks or clipped at the top of their pants.

As I approached the building, I could feel the strong magic intermingled into a complex tapestry. With each person that I passed, I tried to figure out what they were. The only supernaturals distinguishable were shifters because of the ring around their pupil, which was a shade darker than their eyes.

I was greeted as soon as I walked in by the receptionist, an older fae woman. The signs of aging were barely noticeable on her deep mocha skin and nearly white hair that she wore short. Her welcoming smile was done with such ease that I figured she had been there for years—it was as automatic as breathing.

"Ms. Michaels?" Ugh, I didn't like that. The notoriety was going to be a hard thing to deal with, and it being a result of being charged with a crime against supernaturals was even worse. She wasn't asking a question, so I didn't bother to respond. "Mr. Reynolds is expecting you." She looked up at the clock; I was ten minutes late. It was a passive act of aggression. I just really hated being ordered to do something. Would it have hurt for him to ask if I could come down?

She pressed a button and made a call. "She's here." Then she instructed me to go to the fifth floor.

The elevator opened and I was met with just one office that took up the greater part of the floor. Out of my peripheral vision I could see two conference rooms and a restroom, and I leaned in to try to get a better look down the hall.

"Ms. Mich—Levy, come in," Gareth's rich deep voice called from the office. I looked around the minimally furnished space. A large mahogany executive desk, a sofa on the far end of the room with a large table in front and a lamp table on the side furnished the room. He had his own coffee station and a small kitchenette in the back.

"Nice apartment," I said.

He looked around, specifically at the large floor-to-ceiling windows that offered a great view of the city.

"It came with the position. An overkill, I think. Would you like something to drink?"

I shook my head but he didn't seem to see it: once again my outfit was being given a review. "You were at work?" he asked, his brows coming together.

Nice. "It's a laid-back environment. Like this place." I wanted to give his outfit a look of derision, similar to the one he'd given mine, but I couldn't. He looked good. *Damn.* The blue short-sleeved shirt made his oddly blue eyes really stand out, and the dark gray khakis complemented him and his build.

He leaned back against his desk, one arm supporting the other as he stroked his chin, studying me. "Take down your hair."

"What?" I pretended to be surprised and disconcerted by the request. I must have succeeded.

"I smell magic," he said. "Each time you are near I smell it, but you claim to be human."

I shrugged. "I am, but I work around a lot of magical objects." I pulled out an amulet, a piece of pseudomagic that the witches sold to humans. Just a minor spell. Whisper the right word, and it caused a mini explosion like a firecracker. It was crappy magic and even more crappy as a defense tool. Most people knew it was, but kept buying it. Humans seemed to like the idea of using magic to defend themselves or the idea that they had a little bit of it with them. I kept it for times like this.

"You think I haven't been around those things enough to be able to sense them and tell the difference?"

I bit my tongue hard, because I wanted to tell him how little I cared. But once again, that was probably rude.

"Are you always right?"

Another look, slower, and his eyes narrowed as though he was looking through a scope—an assassin's scope. The small kink in his lips was a twisted combination of a smirk and a grin. "The number of times I've been wrong can easily be counted on one hand."

"And he's modest, too," I added under my breath and rolled my eyes. He was a shifter, I knew he heard it. The things that fascinated people about them were the things that bothered me: acute hearing, heightened sense of smell, primal behavior, and skilled hunters. And I could add *arrogant* and possibly *narcissistic* to the list, too.

"Take down your hair," he repeated.

"Why?" I knew exactly why he wanted me to take down my hair. Shields, sigils that blocked others from sensing magic, looked like tattoos. The larger they were, the stronger they were. Most people had them placed on their back, thigh, breast, or anywhere they could be easily hidden, and usually they were utilized by supernaturals who were hiding something—a crime. Like any fugitive, they got a new identity and, like me, pretended to be just human. Shields were unique symbols and definitely a giveaway.

"No." At some point I needed to put my foot down with him. And this was it.

He exhaled a long, slow breath before he spoke. He was someone who wasn't accustomed to being denied and it showed. "Ms. Michaels—"

"Levy. I was found innocent and I don't appreciate you treating me like a criminal."

"No, Miss Michaels, you were found not guilty and I petitioned for you to be released," he said firmly.

"So you think I'm guilty." I backed away. This meeting was starting to go worse than I expected.

"Not at all. But I don't think there's anything innocent about you. They wanted someone to pay for the murders. I want the *right* person to pay. My reputation is on the line here, and I need to know who or what I am working with."

"I told you. Human. I am around magical stuff all the time, I keep a protection gem with me at all times. I don't know my whole lineage." That was a partial truth. I knew enough about it to definitely know I was a Legacy. The moment he found out, I wasn't walking out of here. "I don't know, maybe someone in my family was witch, fae, or mage. For all I know I could have shifter in me."

"Ms. Mi—Levy, since the Cleanse, that is highly unlikely, but let's say I entertain that theory. I sense magic. I need to make sure you aren't actively hiding anything. So prove it," he demanded with a scowl.

"No. I have nothing to prove. You can take my word or not, I don't care." I started toward the door.

"I'll have you arrested," he said before I could even get there. Fastened on me were determined and unwavering eyes.

His cocky and indomitable disposition poked at my irritation and got the best of me. "Why? Because I dared to tell you no? Maybe people should tell you it more often and then you won't be so offended when it happens."

"I'll have you arrested for murder. Last night another one was committed in the same manner as the ones you were arrested for, except a witch was involved. You were released several hours before they occurred, and I have it on good authority that you met with Humans First. So shall we try this again? Take. Down. Your. Hair."

I was fuming. Not just at his request, but because it all made me look suspicious. This was more than coincidence; was someone setting me up? I yanked the tie out of my hair and unraveled the bun. Sliding my fingers through it to get the kinks out, I leaned forward, allowing the strands to slowly cascade through them. If I had a shield on my head, there would have been a noticeable bald spot. Once I was done, I stood up. He was closer than before.

"Apple?"

"What?" My tone was harder and coarser than I'd like. I didn't want to spend time fighting with Gareth, especially since it didn't seem likely I would win. The short time I'd spent with him, it was obvious that he was probably a good ally, but a horrible enemy. I would play nice. "What apple?"

"Your shampoo." He could still smell shampoo from this morning? I tried to determine which trumped the others: creepy, impressive, or scary. It was an impressively scary creepy thing to be good at. *Nailed it.*

"Yeah." I gathered my hair into a ponytail. After a few more moments, he eventually took a step back.

"The shifter that I saw yesterday watching me, was he part of the Guild?"

His brows drew together, his eyes a little cooler as he spoke, his voice slightly edgy. "No, part of the Felidae Clan. They don't believe you are innocent. And since it was one of their own killed that night, I warn you to stay away from them. They are prepared to exact their own brand of justice."

"Okay." Things couldn't have gotten worse. Humans First and the Felidae Clan thought I was guilty. The Magic Council didn't think I was innocent. And I wasn't sure about the mages and the fae. I was in a bad situation, especially with four more murders just an hour after my release. The headache from stress was just a minor ache earlier; now it was raging. How the hell was I going to get out of this mess?

He went behind his desk and rolled the chair next to me. "Take off your shoes."

Fuck.

I was screwed. My shield was on my foot, and stretched from midfoot to my heel. While most people tried to hide theirs within a tapestry of body art, I'd put mine on my foot. Or rather my mom had, along with having it tattooed flesh color. I inspected it often. It was unnoticeable to me, but

Gareth, whose senses were heightened to creepy level, could possibly detect it.

I kept cursing over and over. Prepared to make a scene and walk out. But would he have me arrested? Probably. Once again I'd be at the Haven, in their screwed-up system. I wouldn't be better off, because he could look there.

I took a moment before I moved. Inhaled several easy breaths, trying to calm my erratic heartbeat and breathing. A quick scan of the room and I developed an exit plan, and I was nearly positive it wouldn't work without me using magic. This was how I was going to be exposed: recently released from jail after being suspected of murders that required strong magic—my type of magic—in the Supernatural Guild, by one of the strongest shifters in the country. Or so I assumed, but I couldn't imagine that position would have been given to anyone that they considered mediocre. *Mediocre* didn't hold positions like this. And *mediocre* didn't hold a position on the Magic Council.

Consternation and sorrow settled heavily on me and shallow breaths were all I could manage as I plopped into the chair. I took off my shoes slowly, each moment a countdown to the end, and showed him my left foot. It was on my right. After careful inspection, he looked up. "Why is your heart beating fast?"

"I don't know!" I snapped. It was getting harder and harder to play nice with his freaking odd shifter senses. "When people treat me like a criminal, it's hard for me to relax."

He was sturdily built, but in this position if I kicked him, he would at least lose his balance, giving me some space. I could make it out the door, but there was no way I could make the front door. We were on the fifth floor. I could leave out the window. I was sure the moment I attempted to escape, the building would be locked down. I was screwed.

He remained silent while he finished looking and then waited until I presented the right foot. He kept looking at me. The tension crept over me, the fear, which I was sure he could sense, probably smell. Fear brought magic, the need to protect myself, and I could feel it pulsing in me, unfurling, ready to be released in a hell-storm. I pressed my fingers into my hands, trying to calm it. Each time he looked up, I tried to read his expression, which hadn't changed. He dropped my foot and stood very slowly.

Say something. Do something. I needed feedback.

"Thank you. You may go now."

Relief. I think. For years I wondered if I could pass if I were ever found. Yeah, the Felidae Clan was ready to exact their brand of justice, I was pretty sure the fae and mages weren't too happy with me, and someone was possibly setting me up for murder, but for a brief moment I felt relief.

"I appreciate your cooperation." Leaning against the desk, he dismissed me with a look.

I scoffed as I headed for the door. "Yeah, my cooperation didn't have anything to do with the threat of incarceration."

"You are a stubborn one. You require more incentive to behave. That's on you, not me. I hope cooperation next time doesn't require a threat beforehand." His cool tone was patronizing enough to stop me in my tracks before I could get to the door. I stopped and spun on my heels to face him. Once again, he was relaxed against his desk, with a little devilish smile—far too satisfied with himself. He might have been new to the role of head of the Supernatural Guild, but he seemed to have settled into his position of power with ease. *Look at that,* arrogant, narcissistic, *and I get to add* smug *to the list, too.*

I wasn't moving. I handled the threat of incarceration with more diplomacy than I thought I was capable of. His smugness I tolerated, and his narcissism bothered me, but I could learn to deal with them. His little lecture on my behavior bothered me, however. *He* bugged me, and there was a part of me itching to let him know. A smile pulled at my lips, cloying and exaggerated. "Well, I hope this is the last time we actually need to deal with each other, so it is irrelevant whether I am cooperative or not," I said, before turning and leaving.

His hearty, dark laugh drifted down that hall.

I tried not to think of Gareth's laugh of condescension as I walked, searching my phone for information about the recent murders. Twenty minutes later, I was behind a building's alleyway, where the murders were committed. The smell of garbage overwhelmed the tight space. The blood had been washed away, but some was ingrained in the pores of the concrete. Someone had performed magic, and it was strong. Very strong, different from anything I'd felt. Again, they'd killed a fae, a shifter, a mage, and now a witch. Why the witch? And how the hell did they get them all in the same location to do it? However they did it, they probably used the same thing on me. Four more murders. A witch was the only thing different. I used magic, but I didn't know how to perform many spells. My parents were apprehensive about teaching anything other than the ones they thought could protect me. Magic could help me protect myself, and on the off chance I actually used it, it couldn't always be linked to me. But a spell? If the person were skilled enough it could be traced back to the wielder. That's how the Legacy were discovered and the curse that changed the world as we all knew it had been performed. If someone were to be optimistic, the Cleanse was responsible for bringing the humans and supernaturals together to destroy one common enemy—

us. They destroyed Empyrean, the city where we lived, separate from the world with powerful magic, behind veils and wards. Rarely interacting with others outside of it. We were the magical elite, ancient, strong, and pure magic. We were the magic that existed before it was changed, creating a pale imitation of what we were.

Obsession with power, the desire to rule others was our downfall. Magic against magic we were superior, but then the world toppled under my ancestors' wrongdoing—a spell to rid the world of all magic except our own, we quickly realized. I hated that I used *we*. Because *we* didn't do it, my parents didn't do it, their well-intentioned friends didn't do it. They fought to prevent the spell, most of them killed while doing so. My parents survived, barely escaping in time before the war began, but were still held guilty by association. Just as I was guilty by association. And I doubted if I promised on a stack of holy books, pinky-swore, took a Girl Scout oath, or made a declaration of intent that I would never ever, ever, ever do a spell that would kill all things that possessed magic while I hid behind a ward impervious to its devastation, anyone would believe me.

The deep, guttural rumble coming from the end of the alleyway pulled me from my thoughts. A compact, muscled jaguar padded slowly toward me. I took several steps back. It pulled back its lips, exposing fangs. Deadly fangs. I'd left my meeting with Gareth and come straight to the location of the murders. The only thing I had on me for defense was the witch protection charm. Knowing its limited capabilities, I would have to get close enough to the animal to get to its face or neck. A small burn near it would at the very least slow it down and maybe I could get away. I did a quick scan of the area to find another weapon to assist. Nothing.

Slowly I stepped back, and it snarled as it moved faster toward me. The path of the confined space narrowed as I got closer to the Dumpsters. I gave the alley another sweeping look, trying to find something to use as a weapon. There were small shards of broken glass but nothing big enough to be of any use. Discarded boxes that had missed landing in the bin. Once again—useless. I grabbed the broken umbrella that was close to the opposite end of the alley. I just needed something. Grabbing it as I continued back, I realized running wasn't an option and I was close to Trace Lane, a heavily populated cat shifter territory. It wasn't something I'd considered when I came to investigate the area.

Just a few feet away, it reared back on its legs, ready to leap. I tried to anticipate its movement, hoping it would try to bite. I could shove the umbrella in its mouth. If it tried to get me with its claws, I would have to be fast enough to side-step. It lunged at me. A body flashed past me and grabbed the animal by the throat, midleap, noticeably expelling a hard breath as it hit the ground with a thud.

"Change." Gareth growled his command to the jaguar. It didn't do anything. "I said change, or this is going to be a very unfortunate situation for you. Do it now."

I stared at the person who was only cloaked in Gareth's body. He was deadly, scary, and a force I didn't want to mess with. Violence wafted off him, and even with my limited senses I could feel it goading every self-protective part of me. If I could feel it, so could the jaguar, who melted into his human form, just as stocky and stealthy-looking as his animal. I couldn't see his face. Gareth was still over him but had relaxed his stranglehold on his neck. But the Guild head was positioned in a manner that made it apparent he was ready to strike again at any moment.

"I need you to listen to me very carefully. She's innocent. Do not insult me or the Council by questioning our decision. The person responsible will be found. Going after her will not help the situation. Pass it on: an attack against her is an attack against me." He released the gentleman. He came to standing. His eyes blazed with anger and his features squared off more as his jaw clenched. He breathed so hard out of his nose, it reminded me of a bull before he was about to charge.

"Are we clear?" Gareth asked.

It took him a moment to answer, and when he did, his voice was calmer than I expected. "Fine." Without another word he turned and walked away as naked as the day he was born, with probably less shame.

Anyone who wandered around near Trace Lane was so used to seeing naked bodies traipsing about it lost its allure.

"Didn't I say to stay away from the cats?" Gareth asked.

"Are you following me?"

"No, I'm not. By the way, you're welcome."

I mumbled a thank-you. "I had it under control."

He looked down at the umbrella. "Of course, when I'm trying to take down a jaguar, I always bring an umbrella," he scoffed and shrugged. "After all, how else do you fight one?"

"It's the only weapon I could find." I felt a little silly clinging to it and it had to look even sillier. "We can't all use our position as head of the Supernatural Guild to scare people into compliance," I shot back, tossing the umbrella toward the bin.

"Yeah, it was my position that made him change his mind." Once again I was treated to a little kink in his lips: his typical smirk of derision.

Slipping past me, he started walking the length of the alleyway, frowning when he got closer to a trash bin. If I could smell the foul odor wafting off it, I knew he could. He knelt down, near where I saw the blood in the crevices of the street.

"The Necro-spear was stolen," he informed me in a tight voice.

"When?"

"The same night we found you. We suspect it was used to kill the shifters."

Once again, I was linked to the murders. It was in our possession at one time, and I knew the Supernatural Guild had it. Whoever stole it broke the mage ward protecting it. Wards could be made by both witches and mages. The locals usually had them done by witches—it was cheaper, and met most people's basic needs. Humans bought them mostly for bragging rights, to have access to a magical ward that could make magic appear and disappear with just the use of an invocation given to them by a witch.

"What do you think is going on?"

"I have no idea." His appealing features pulled into a tightly formed moue. He'd withdrawn into his thoughts. This wasn't a man who didn't have an idea. It was a man who had an idea but didn't want to voice it, as though saying it made it more real. Or perhaps saying it was painful.

"Any speculations?" I asked.

The silence stretched. "We both want to find out who is doing this. Maybe our reasons are different, but we have a common goal," I said, reading his reluctance to divulge information.

"You're willing to help?"

"Anything you need."

"Good." He started away from the alleyway. "Do you need to go back to work?"

I looked at the time on my phone. I had been gone for three hours. And I was sure the box I'd left Kalen with wasn't the only one he had to go through. Kalen had probably given up on me. And looking at the three urgent messages, he not only had given up on me, he was panicking. It had to be bad for business to have an employee arrested for murder.

I sent him a message letting him know I was on my way.

"Hurry, you have a visitor."

"Who?"

"*Clive?*" he responded, with a fire emoji.

"Not so hot. Part of Humans First."

I knew that would get the frowny face, and seconds later he sent several.

I started toward the bus stop; it was going to take me at least another half hour to get back to work.

"I can give you a ride," Gareth offered. I looked at the white AMG, a different car than he'd had at Crimson, and down at the bus stop. Back at the car and then the bus stop again. I'd have liked to think it was an easy decision. The fact that it wasn't, if I were him, would have made me rescind the offer, but he seemed to find it amusing. I still hadn't made a decision when he walked over to the driver's side and opened the door. "Get in."

Another long, lingering look at the bus stop, and then my gaze followed the arriving bus before I got into the car. The nicest car I'd been in was Kalen's black Audi, which he operated like he was trying to drive fast enough to defy physics and go back in time.

Gareth was a little more cautious, but not much. He weaved and darted in and out of traffic, then he looked over, grinned, and slowed the car down. "Sorry."

"It's fine, I was almost eaten by a jaguar, why not add heart attack to it?" The car slowed to a crawl, creeping along the road below the speed limit. I didn't say anything because it was probably bothering him more to drive that slowly than me. *I'll play your game, Gareth.*

"Were you serious about wanting to help?"

My head barely moved into the nod.

"I think if we can retrieve the missing memory of the night we found you, it will be helpful."

"And you plan on doing that how?"

"I know a witch, very talented and very strong."

I tensed, noticeably feeling the same anxiety I had when he searched me. I didn't want a witch rooting around in my head. And definitely not a talented one. But I guessed a novice wasn't any better. "You trust her?"

It didn't matter. "When?"

"Tomorrow."

Again my head barely moved into the nod, I was preoccupied with the city that crept by. Ironically we passed by Coven Row, which was just a small group of shops owned by witches. You could get anything from an elusive love spell to wards and protection charms. Some were nothing more than glamorized holistic shops and I questioned whether the owners were even witches. Seriously, chakra-centering candles? They weren't even trying.

But I loved the area. It reminded me of the French Quarter. Eclectic bright colors, frilly lace, and plants that curved around the windows and doors. If you were looking for a love spell, they were the first place to look. If a person wanted a guide down their life path or a view of their other life, they'd check the gothic-looking one. It was a deep red building, with room-darkening blinds. Instead of lovely decorations on the door, there were vines wrapping around the outside and interwoven through it. And you could buy herbs, which was where they made most of their money. Hemp being illegal and all, it was funny that a witch could sell *herba terrae*, or earth plant, their magical herb that smelled a lot like it. Those shops did the best. Then there were the simple shops, with magic spell books, candles, and anything that one might need to perform a spell, which had no chance of working if the person wasn't magically inclined. But most humans kept coming back, hoping it would wake some dormant magical ability they were convinced they possessed.

Some humans had ancestors who might have possessed

magic, but throughout the years of mating with humans, the magic had been diluted to the point that it wasn't enough for them to be considered supernatural. Unfortunately, it was enough for the Legacy magic during the Cleanse to bind to it and kill them.

"What time are we going to see her?" I asked.

"What time do you get off work?"

"Pick me up at seven."

It was later than I usually got off, but I needed to see if I could do something to get the information before I handed my head and memories over to a witch.

"Pick you up here or at your home?"

"Home." I started to give him the address but stopped. I was sure he already had it.

As soon as the car came to a complete stop, I thanked him and padded up the stairs. The last thing I needed him to know was that Mr. Humans First was at my job waiting for me. That seemed to have *fight* written all over it.

Clive was sitting back in a chair relaxing in the waiting room, or what most people would refer to as the living room, the odd benefit of working in a home/business. He had an unopened bottle of water on the small table next to him and was scrolling through his phone. When I walked in, he sat up taller and smiled. He didn't look like he belonged in a spy movie at all today. He wore a relaxed white shirt and a pair of jeans. In the light his hair didn't look as dark and the various hues of brown were more noticeable, along with his eyes. They were gentler, but keen, sweeping over me briefly before they returned to his phone. His thumbs swept over the keys, I assumed sending a message that the eagle had landed or some silly phrase they probably used.

Off from the living room/sitting area was a kitchen. That was where Kalen stood, sipping on a bottle of water with a smile so fake plastered on he reminded me of a ventriloquist's dummy. He'd most likely mustered the saccharine grin the moment I'd told him Clive was a member of HF. The look broke as soon as he took a look at my hair. He pointed to his head, frowned, and shrugged. His way of asking, "What the hell is going on with your hair?" He did it so often all he had to do was frown and point and I knew what he was thinking. I'd seen my coiffure earlier in the car with Gareth. It was bad after he searched it, and my run-in with the jaguar hadn't made it any better. Once again Kalen shot me his look of scorn. On any given day, I didn't know what we were doing, so I dressed for it. He, on the other hand, dressed like we were going to a business dinner and he had clients to impress. It was absolutely amusing watching his face when he helped me wade through garbage, or go through the stolen goods in an abandoned warehouse, or even worse, on one of the farms outside of the city, where we had to go into a barn, attic, or even better yet, a small pond to retrieve a magical object. All the while he'd complain about ruining his Tom Ford clothing. But since I'd worked for him, I hadn't seen him wear anything else. Not even a pair of jeans and a shirt. I once gave a pair to him for his birthday.

"Clive, what do you need?" I finally asked after my brief nonverbal conversation with Kalen.

"I wanted to finish our conversation from yesterday." He came to his feet and a smile settled over his face as though the conversation we'd had the night before hadn't been resolved.

"Me telling you I wasn't interested warranted another visit?" I shrugged. "I'm not interested. Bye." I opened the front door for him, mindful of Kalen, who relaxed into his smile, his magic gently gliding throughout the room, saturating the air, pent-up balls of it ready to be released. It did that when he was upset. He was more than upset now, and if Clive could feel magic, sense the subtle changes in it, feel the rise of defensive magic ready to be used, he wouldn't be displaying such confidence. It crowded the room. One baleful look in Kalen's direction and it inched back, folding under his control. Kalen was convinced I could tell he was doing magic because I could see the changes in his face, and I didn't correct him. I'd become so comfortable around him, sometimes things slipped and I had to remind myself that being comfortable and relaxed wasn't an option—not with anyone.

Kalen couldn't use magic against Clive. It was what HF wanted to believe—the supernaturals were wild, unchecked people with dangerous power at their fingertips. It didn't matter to them that magic was regulated, with rules and consequences. The rules weren't rigid enough and the consequences not harsh enough for HF.

"Please, let's have lunch and discuss it more."

I glanced at the clock on the wall. "It's too late for lunch."

"Fine. Dinner?"

"I have to work." I looked at Kalen and gave him a look. *Say something.*

His stance was relaxed, his typical quiescent demeanor well under control. He smiled. "No, it's fine. You can leave. Tomorrow we'll start early."

He simply ignored my dirty look, but I wanted him to get a view of it up close and personal. I excused myself and went to the back office, beckoning Kalen to follow.

"What is wrong with you?" I asked in a low voice through clenched teeth.

"He's persistent and he's not going to leave you alone. For whatever reason he wants you, isn't it a good idea to see what they have brewing? As bad as he seems to want you as a member, I'm sure you can get more information. Worst case, you learn nothing and get a nice dinner out of the deal with a hot, misguided malcontent. Best-case scenario, you get enough information to cause the Supernatural Guild or the police to take notice. I personally don't think HF is as harmless as people would like to believe."

"So you are pimping me out for dinners. Are you proud of yourself?"

He gave me another sweeping look and made a face. "Dinner's probably all I'm going to get for you. What happened to your hair? And why do you look like you've been fighting vampires?"

"I wish it were vampires." Since I wasn't in a rush to have dinner with Clive, I gave him the extended version of the story. Gareth threatening to put me in jail, his inspection, which I was pretty sure was an illegal one, the fact that the Cat Clan considered me guilty and wanted to do something about it, the near attack by the jaguar, Gareth's intervention and his request for me to see a witch to retrieve my lost memories. Just telling it made me exhausted.

I'd expected him to shrug off Gareth's suspicions with a snarky response, but he didn't. Instead he had withdrawn into his thoughts. A moment of silence became minutes, and a furrowed brow and deeply set frown overtook his face. "Are you?"

"Am I what?"

"Some form of magic." My chest tightened; the guilt of lying to a friend, someone I trusted, always did that to me. Kalen had lost people during the Cleanse and his family suffered. Would he ever trust me? Would things be the same? And wouldn't I be putting him at risk of punishment if he didn't expose me?

"Of course not." I walked toward Clive. Fae weren't allowed to compel people to truth or manipulate their minds the same way vampires weren't. It was force, mind rape. Consent had to be given. Although, like vampires, fae's physical beauty made compelling and love spells unnecessary, it was still illegal to perform them.

The inquiring look remained on his face. Something I hadn't seen before. Gareth's suspicions had become Kalen's doubt.

Another point against Gareth.

Clive declined going to the coffeehouse near the office and instead wanted to walk. For several blocks, each time I looked in his direction, I found him assessing me. We passed several restaurants, and Clive stopped at one and looked at the menu. I didn't like how comfortable he was with me. Or the confident way his arm reached around my back and pulled me to him as he looked at the menu. What bothered me the most was how at ease and comfortable he was with his hand pressed against my back, guiding me to the next restaurant. It was too familiar, as though we were buddies, friends, two people casually taking a midday stroll and finding a good place to have a meal. From everything I knew about him and HF, we were two people on opposite sides of an issue. For some foolish reason he was convinced he could bring me over to his side. I wasn't sure what about me gave him the impression that I could be swayed so easily to hate people just because of the way they were born. After a few more minutes of walking, nearly five blocks from the office, he found a Mexican restaurant that piqued his interest. Various smells of onion and spiced meat reminded me that the only thing I had eaten all day was a croissant from the coffeehouse.

It wasn't until we walked into the restaurant that I started to feel the hunger pangs and my empty stomach growled. We were seated in a small booth at the back of the restaurant and Clive watched me as I looked over the menu. He ordered two large margaritas, as a way to lower my inhibitions. It was easy to forget he was an arrogant narcissist as I sat across from him. The curious smile blossomed and faded each time I looked up from the menu. Once tortilla chips and salsa arrived, I scarfed down half the basket before he spoke.

"So what is the Haven like?" he asked, taking a sip of his drink.

"I'm sure they are willing to give you a tour if you ask for one." I took a drink from my water instead of the margarita.

"You don't like me, do you?" His voice was soft, velvety smooth and gentle, an induction into a song and dance in which he would take the lead. Moving me rhythmically over his lyrics of persuasion. I was sure this wasn't his first dance. He was probably a pro.

"It doesn't matter whether I like you or not. This is a business dinner, right?"

He spread his arms out, relaxing against the back of the booth and slipping down into the cushions, and once again I had his undivided attention. "I was hoping it could be more."

"I'm sorry it's not. You wanted to talk about HF. Go ahead." Clive was a distraction, and I could tell he was more than aware of his charm, looks, and the enchanting. But I wasn't going to fall for it, because behind those gentle eyes was a menace. I didn't doubt for one moment that if he ever found out who I was, I would no longer be looking at the face of a handsome man trying to recruit me to HF, but instead a person who would be my killer.

"I heard about you taking down two vampires without even killing them. I didn't believe the stories until I witnessed you at the club."

"How ironic—a member of HF hanging out at a vampire club."

"I do believe you have HF wrong. We don't have a problem with supernaturals. I just think that they need to be regulated better. And more boundaries between us and them would improve safety."

"How can they be regulated more? They have their own police and strict laws that could even end in death for some infractions. Besides, most crimes committed aren't by supernaturals."

He chuckled and took another sip from his glass before he leaned into the table. The restaurant was darker than outside and the pale lights were reflected in a glint in his eyes as they fastened on me.

"I don't for one minute think you're that naïve. You know that the Magic Council goes to great lengths to hide their infractions and make them look a lot more innocent and innocuous than they are. Your friend was attacked by a vampire; do you think that is acceptable?"

"He wasn't acting on his own," I pointed out in a cool, severe voice. Any other time I might try to soften it, but I wanted to make it clear that I wasn't interested.

The restaurant was starting to get a little bit crowded. Conversation blended with the soft music, the bustle of waitstaff walking back and forth from the kitchen, and the light buzz I was getting from the margarita were all becoming a distraction. I didn't need a distraction. I needed to be aware. Hyperaware.

"Then isn't that even more concerning? Someone was controlling vampires."

The waiter dropped off our food: a chimichanga for me and a couple of soft tacos for him. Clive ordered two more margaritas; I changed the order to one, just for him. Mine was nearly full. My inhibitions and wit were still intact, the way they needed to be, dealing with him.

He took a bite and between chewing said, "People think that the Cleanse was a bad thing; I don't."

I sighed. He didn't take long getting to the same rhetoric I had seen in their pamphlets and heard when the news covered their rallies and meetings. They weren't very big, but every once in a while, someone did something disruptive and it would make news. They touted themselves as being a peaceful organization, but they had a very archaic and ominous view. He was silent for a while, allowing me to contemplate and consider his words.

"We were wrong to intervene."

It was at that moment I considered just packing up my food, downing my drink, and heading out the door. He knew nothing of the Cleanse. For people like him, it was glamorized. They didn't see the curse that drifted throughout the city, attaching to anything magical, sucking it out of them and claiming their life. A path of destruction in its wake. It started with the weakest, those who didn't demonstrate any magical skills or abilities or were vaguely aware that they had them. Pure humans were left untouched, but they watched their fallen brothers and sisters who'd lived in ignorance without the knowledge that they were part supernatural. Humans had been afraid that they could be next. And as the curse coursed throughout the land, it killed off the lower-level witches, mages, and fae, leaving only the strong. But the strongest supernaturals were the targets and the very people whom the Legacy wanted destroyed in the first place. People like Clive and his followers didn't realize that the Legacy wanted the strongest gone so they could have total power. HF's misguided members were seduced by this Utopian world where people didn't shift into animals, immortal creatures that drank blood didn't exist, and magic was just something found in a book of fairy tales. They weren't aware that eventually the humans would have become slaves.

He put his elbow on the table, resting his chin on his hand as he looked at me with renewed curiosity. "What's the matter?"

I lifted my glass and took another sip. "This is stronger than I thought."

Anger, resentment, and frustration burned in my belly. It all felt like a shawl that wrapped around me too tightly. Although I wasn't there, I could remember the story, each time my mother told me, and the sadness in her eyes. I remembered the way they glistened from unshed tears, the rasp in her voice, and the streaks of color that rose over her neck and her cheeks as if she was reliving it again. Back in Empyrean, where Legacy lived, a place now destroyed by bombs and strong magic.

"Levy, we aren't the only ones that feel that way. There are even those in the supernatural community who want to see some changes. Things are in the works, change is coming. Don't get lost within it."

As a recruiter he was very good at his job, and maybe it worked on a lot of people, but I was tired of this conversation. I was tired of reliving memories that I had long buried. I didn't want to sit there and discuss the very reason I couldn't come out of the closet like everyone else. Why I had to live in constant fear of being discovered. I didn't want to play his game anymore. I was done.

"I'm not sure which way you need me to say it, but let me say this in no uncertain terms: I am not interested in joining Humans First. I'm not a sympathizer. I don't understand where you are coming from, and I'll never believe in your rhetoric. Most of the time, I consider you all ridiculous." I looked down at my half-eaten chimichanga, wrapped it in a napkin, and came to my feet. I fought the urge to lean in and tell him about the Cleanse, and all the intentions, and pull a thread out of his tapestry of uninformed adulation for something that was downright cruel and draconian. But I doubted it would change anything. The Cleanse proved one thing: he was a special little snowflake. Pure human. And he and the rest of HF probably wore it like a badge of honor.

"At least let me take you home," he offered as he came to his feet, too.

I simply mumbled a no and headed out the door before he could follow me. I was sure he knew where I lived, but there was no way I would take another meeting with him no matter how persistent he was. But I couldn't help but think, who in the supernatural community felt this way, and how could they?

CHAPTER 9

$\mathcal{I}$ did not have a problem with the long stretch of silence between Gareth and me. A half an hour into the drive, I had relaxed back in the car, listening to the music, surprised by his choice. A unique blend of new age music, rap, and the sultry sound of jazz wasn't what I expected Pandora to be playing. Most of the time I busied myself with the scene outside the window as we drove out of the city and farther into the country. I lived near Chicago; this part of the Midwest was what I considered the forgotten area. The trees dwindled down to large florets of luscious greenery and were slowly starting to show the transition from summer to fall. We passed several miles of cornfields. Small farmhouses sat back from the road with acres of fertile land. And when he drove off the main road, responding to the curious look I gave him, he said, "I have no idea why she wanted us to meet her out here."

"She doesn't live out here?"

"Their coven owns it. They come out here to practice."

Is she going to be practicing her memory retrieval skills on me?

I looked at him, and as though he'd read my thoughts, or

more specifically my face, he offered, "She's really good. It's probably because she wanted privacy."

We drove down the dark pathways to a small red brick ranch house. At one time, it might have been a farm, but the land had been abandoned. Near the house the grass was green, plush, and well maintained; a few feet away was barren land, patches of poorly kept grass and dry soil. Behind the house was a small pond, but it looked empty. Also behind were a few stretches of ground, wired off, with plants growing within. I assumed some of the herbs they used for spells, but some looked like their *herba terrae*.

Gareth knocked one time, opened the door, and peeked his head in as a soft, silky voice welcomed him. The large smile matched the light, spirited tone of her voice. I wasn't sure what I expected—someone older, maybe a little less modern in her dress. Someone who looked like she possessed old-world knowledge. Instead, standing in front of us was a tall slender woman. Her dark, thick masses of curls were too big for her narrow face and were just a couple of shades darker than her walnut-colored skin. In contrast were the tips, which were dyed indigo blue. Large bracelets jingled around her narrow wrists. And her earrings, like her hair, were just a little too large. I wasn't sure if the Jimi Hendrix t-shirt was worn ironically or not. I quickly put her in the "peculiar" category.

"Hi." She greeted Gareth with a hug, and me with a firm handshake. Then she turned her attention to me. "I'm Blu, no *E*, and will be working my witchy skills on you today." She grinned. Okay, she was peculiar as hell and her parents had named her after a color—what wasn't to like?

"Why not the *E*?"

Her response was so automatic that I was sure she'd been asked so many times it didn't even bother her. "You'll have to ask my parents. My dad's a jazz saxophonist, and my mother sings. I'm just happy that they didn't name me Thelonious, Duke, Ella, or Sade. I think Jazz was in the running, too. The artist in them just decided to keep it weird and artsy. So I'm Blu Jasmine. I feel like I should be on stage." She smiled.

I laughed—she made sense. How could she not be peculiar?

"Thanks for coming out here. We're about to migrate to questionable territory and I don't need an audience."

Sweet. I'm about to let a witch perform borderline strong and illegal magic in the woods, away from most of the population. She pulled out a tube and filled it with herbs. She whispered an incantation, and the leaves came alive with vibrant hues of blue, orange, and yellow. Then vapors puffed from the tube's opening.

"Here."

"What do I do with it?"

She chuckled and gave Gareth a look, raising an eyebrow in confusion. "You inhale. It will help you to relax. It'll be easier for me to negotiate your mind."

I sat it on the table, I didn't need to inhale it, the vapors were filling the room. I didn't want any part of it. "No, thank you. Will you put that out?"

"It'll be easier if you try it," she urged. She smiled, and I was sure if I didn't use it, she would.

Once again I declined. I didn't want to be relaxed, I wanted to be guarded. As much as I wanted to retrieve the memory, I was more concerned about what else she would find while rooting around in my head—especially while I was high.

"What about tea?"

"Unless it's green tea, I'll pass."

Again, her eyes lifted to meet Gareth's. I wasn't sure what he did behind me and I didn't care. I wasn't smoking "witch weed" or drinking their witchy tea. I was already allowing her to rummage around in my head; I'd be damned if I gave her free rein while inside of it.

She guided me to a sofa and asked me to sit. She lit several candles around the room, soft scents, vanilla and cinnamon. Like a flower, they quickly filled the room with appealing aromas. Moving over to the curio, she pulled out a couple of things: a charm, salts, and a gray crystal-like substance. She dipped her finger in the gray crystal powder and made a mark on my forehead. The salt was spread around us both, and then she held the charm between both of our hands.

"All you have to do is relax and I'll do everything."

She closed her eyes. I wasn't sure if I needed to, but I followed suit. Her voice dropped to a low, gentle murmur and the words came fast, indiscernible. The charm warmed, and magic, powerful and potent, filled the air, so strong it was almost stifling. A kaleidoscope of colors overtook my vision. Magic danced and whirled around me.

"Just relax and open your mind to me," she said softly, ushering the magic lightly forward.

The magic hit. I wondered why she needed me high to do this. I couldn't be any more relaxed than I was as the pastel rainbow of colors danced around my eyes. Memories flashed in and out, pleasant ones that seemed so far in my past that I'd forgotten them. Lighthearted images that made me smile, some that caused me to laugh. She laughed. *Does she see them, too?*

"Show me the last thing you remember the night before they found you with the bodies," she directed in a soothing voice.

I thought about it and started to tell her.

"You don't need to speak, just think." And I did. Her hand tightened around mine briefly before it was ripped away and she soared through the room, slamming into the wall. She gasped for breath. Something was off. This wasn't her magic. It wasn't witch's magic at all. I grabbed the twins and headed out the door with Gareth right behind me.

A strong magic tornado slammed against me. I stumbled. Magic, different from Blu's, ravaged. I could feel her trying to push against it, but it was too strong—mage magic. A witch would not stand a chance against mage magic. I waited for the mages to reveal themselves, sai in hand, ready to engage. I stepped closer to the woods, feeling the thrashing of magic against the air, its dark presence. I was hit hard by a heavy furry body, warm breath hit my face, and a growl reverberated against my chest. Large fangs drew closer, about to take a bite out of me, when Gareth slammed against it, knocking it off of me. I quickly rolled to my feet. It lunged again, exposing fangs, salivating at the mouth, eyes just as vacant as those of the vampires who'd attacked me at the auction. It wasn't acting on its own; something was control- ling it. When it charged at me again, I slid one of the twins into its side, making sure to hit the belly. I didn't want to kill; it wasn't working on its own. I just needed to protect myself. It whined in pain and crumpled as it hit the ground. It made another attempt to attack. Gareth careened into it and tossed it to the ground; with a tie in hand, he secured its limbs. It was done so quickly and with such ease it was obvious he'd done this many times before. Before he could move the animal, I saw four more approaching us. They padded slowly at first, but quickly transitioned into a full run, charging at us.

"You take the one on the right, and I'll take the other three," he commanded.

Even during a fight he was egotistical and arrogant. He was going to take three? But I didn't have time to say anything before he pulled out his phone, pressed a button, and said, "I'm going to need a cleanup." He tossed the phone out of the way, and I assumed they were going to use the locator on the phone to find us.

"Try not to kill them if you can help it. Someone is controlling them."

Thank you, Captain Obvious.

He took several steps back as an animal lunged toward him. Gareth started toward him at a speed that looked almost as if he'd taken flight, and then he changed, sprouting into a massive feline, tawny thick coat stretched over the thick muscled limbs that moved with grace and ferocity. His massive fangs extended like daggers. I didn't know if I could even call it a tiger because creatures like him didn't roam the earth anymore. A large majestic creature that had been reduced to something as pedantic as *feline*, but there weren't many other words to define him. He was feline in its most primal, ancient existence. The large cat before me could very well belong in prehistoric times with the dire wolves, saber-toothed tigers, and mammoths, and survived. With his massive paw, he smacked the challenger across the air, sending it cannoning several feet away. The creature started to get up but then collapsed. I didn't have time to see what else happened because a large wolf approached me. Its massive weight had me by at least a hundred and fifty pounds. If it slammed into me or landed on me, I was done. I took a couple of steps back, needing enough distance to run and make a maneuver around it. Thirty feet away I started to run toward it. The creature charged, galloping fast, and I quickly sidestepped and punched a sai into its side. It wailed. I pulled it out and did it again, shoving it between its ribs, enough to cause pain but not collapse the lung. It gasped for breath. I wanted to make sure it couldn't get up and attack again. I moved behind it and let one of the sai slide into its Achilles tendon. It fell to the ground and when it attempted to stand, it crashed down again. Shifters healed fast. He'd be pissed today and in substantial pain, but fine in a day or two. By the time I finished, Gareth was walking toward me in human form—naked. I looked away, but not before seeing him grin as I tried not to look.

It wasn't like I hadn't seen a naked shifter before. In fact, if you went through heavily shifter-populated areas, it was rare that you left without seeing a naked body crossing the street going toward the woods to change, or coming out of them after they had changed. Shapeshifters were not known for being modest in any way. Often very gifted with physiques that didn't make you turn away, they didn't possess a sliver of the shame that most people had about their own nudity. And Gareth seemed to be very much the same. I wasn't sure how much time had passed, but three cars and a van pulled up as he walked to his car. He was putting on a pair of pants when a man walked up to him.

"What are we doing with them?" the guy asked.

"They will need medical attention. Once they are healed, I need them to be available for questioning."

Gareth went over to the crew and started giving orders before he headed toward the house. I followed behind him; when we entered, Blu was lying on the floor. Her head lolled to the side, her skin pallid and eyes closed. Magic still lingered in the air and the herbs mingled with it.

He knelt down next to her and asked, "Are you okay?"

She attempted to roll to sitting but quickly decided against it and lay back down. After a few minutes she tried again, taking his hand as he helped her to standing. He steadied her as she started to sway back. "That was a hell of a punch." She attempted to smile but seemed too weak to fully commit to it. Several moments passed before he seemed to be confident that she could stand on her own. He took several steps away. At the same time they both looked at my arm. When her eyes widened, it was the first time I actually looked at it.

The pain had wrapped around my arm and the constant intensity of it had made me numb to it. Blood ran down it, the skin open from where claws had raked across it. I couldn't remember when it happened. With the endorphins gone and the adrenaline high slaked, the throbbing was noticeable. A deep thump that felt like someone was plucking at my nerves like a string instrument and beating on my muscles like a drum. I clenched my jaw. The numbed state was over and the pain came back—hard. It was nearly unbearable. I didn't know which one hurt more: a vampire bite or shapeshifter's scratch. I was quite ashamed I knew what they both felt like and the experiences had come within the span of a week.

"Let me do a healing spell," Blu offered, taking my arm. She wavered a little, and Gareth was at her side in seconds.

"Are you strong enough?" he asked.

Moving in slow, measured steps, each one looking painful and difficult, she examined the arm. "I will not be able to heal it completely, I am just too weak, but I can definitely keep her from going to the Isles."

Oh, that place again. Again something I hadn't experienced until this week. She continued to hold my arm and directed Gareth to get the supplies. He lit the candle, she marked the area with a creamy substance, and then with a simple invocation, the skin drew together, a light mess of connected tissue formed over it, a fresh layer of skin left in its place. And it cooled, reducing the throbbing to a light, tolerable ache.

She slumped against the wall. Her voice was light and wispy, barely audible. "I can't do any more. Can you come back tomorrow when I'm stronger?"

Although I agreed, I didn't think it was a good idea. Obviously someone didn't want her to help me retrieve that memory. The big question was who and why. I bet if I followed the trail to who, I'd find out the why. Just as I did at the Haven, I started cataloging all the ways I wanted to make them pay for doing this to me.

Gareth helped her up and took her out of the room. He was so gentle as he handled her, it made me think that they were probably more than just friends. When he left the room, I busied myself with looking at all the things around it. The various herbs, charms, and dozens of spell books in the bookcases that lined the walls. I took note of all the symbols that marked the walls and were probably wards. Strong enough to keep a weaker mage out and other witches and even fae, but not a strong mage and definitely not a shifter. And that was strong mage magic that I'd felt. After Jonathan's stunt the other day, I knew what it felt like. You only needed to feel magic once to be able to identify it—at least by type. I'd been around Kalen so much that I could identify fae magic easily. With the exception of the mage Tracker I'd encountered a year ago, I hadn't actively been around mage magic. What mage was involved, and why had they set me up? How were they controlling shapeshifters? The Legacy were the only ones who had the power to do so, and I was the only Legacy in the city. Could there be someone else with the ability? Another supernatural? I considered all the possibilities. Like all things, magic went through evolutionary changes. Had mages' abilities evolved to include necromancy? Or had necromancers' magic advanced to not only have rule over the dead, but animals as well?

Gareth didn't seem entirely convinced when I told him I thought a mage was involved. We'd managed to wash some of the blood off before leaving the witch's house. But there were still traces of it on us. We needed showers.

"Why do you think it's a mage?"

"Because if Blu is as strong as you say she is, there is no way she shouldn't have been able to counter the attack."

I couldn't tell him that the magic I'd felt was similar to Jonathan's. Then I realized that Gareth could scent magic but wasn't able to type it, which was good for me. However, it wouldn't have been any use if he could if he'd never encountered a Legacy; he would never be able to pinpoint the magic. He would only know what type of magic it wasn't.

He sat in silent contemplation, his strongly hewn features clenched as he drove down the streets.

"By the way, nice … lion?" I said, looking in his direction, still having a difficult time accepting the type of animal he'd turned into.

"You've never seen a lion before?" His lips twisted sardonically, and his gaze flashed in my direction. The shifter ring around his eyes twinkled indigo.

"I've seen a lion before. I've seen a lion shifter before, too. What you turned into was the unholy union of a lion and a dragon."

"Wouldn't I have scales and breathe fire?"

"Okay, a lion and a big bear?"

"What type of bear? A lion is larger than some bears."

I chuckled. "Okay, lion and elephant."

"Did you see a trunk?" His voice was mocking.

I expelled an exasperated breath. "I don't want to play guess-the-mutated-cat with you. Why are you so damn big?"

A deep chuckle reverberated in his chest, and a smile bloomed. "Well, that definitely is not the first time a woman has asked me that, either."

I pressed my lips into a thin line and forced silence, trying to ignore the amusement he found in his salacious joke. It didn't help. "Dirty jokes from Mr. Head of Supernatural Guild and Almighty Magical Council Member?"

"You flatter me. I think I'm a lot less important than you've made me out to be. But, I must point out, you made it dirty. I pointed out an observation," he said, hitting me with yet another sinful grin.

He was quite the wordsmith. Refusing to be redirected, I continued with my questioning. "You're not a lion, so what are you?"

"*Panthera leo spelaea*, or in layman's terms, cave lion."

I let the words roll around in my head before I said, "Those are extinct."

He shrugged, shooting a teasing look in my direction. But I was trying to focus on the view outside because I caught myself focusing too much on the view inside—him. "Okay, then what you saw was just a figment of your imagination. That's why I never believe things are extinct. I'm proof of it. If I ever see that dinosaur, I'll let you know."

Gareth took a route to my house that I wasn't familiar with, and when he passed the exit to my apartment, I asked, "Where are we going?"

"I can't possibly take you home looking like that. I don't believe I received anything less than ten calls a day from Savannah when you were at the Haven. And thanks for telling her that I threatened to jail you. The only thing worse than an attorney is their kid. She doesn't seem to grasp that the rules are different. She is tenacious."

"Try living with her. Have you ever had kale chips? Yeah, that's a treat in my home. And she keeps trying to get me to join the Bikram cult."

"That's yoga."

I looked in his direction, my eyes suspicious. "They got to

you, too. All I know is that she goes there every day and when she comes home she has a strange look in her eyes. She forsakes all just to go to their meetings. She worships at the feet of the idol Lululemon. You say yoga, and I say cult."

He laughed, and again I found myself staring at him. And once again I pulled my attention from him and focused on something else. The new surroundings that I hadn't seen before. An area of the city that I hadn't been to. Just when I was about to ask where we were going, he made a turn, drove to a gate, and swiped a card. We wound around a vacant curvy street, passing blocks of sylvan groves.

"Where are we?"

"My home. You can clean up and get some food and we can talk about today."

"Shouldn't you be doing that with the people at the Guild?"

He studied me for a moment, long and hard. Then he frowned, deep creases forming around his brow and lips. He rubbed his fingers over his lips and more time passed before he spoke. "I can do both. At what point should I be offended that you hate being around me?"

"*Hate* is a pretty strong word. Call me crazy, but I have a problem being around people who threaten to lock me up."

"I've only threatened once." He dismissed my point with a wave of his hand. "Ms. Michaels, you seem to be in the middle of this case. Everything leads to you, so I do believe it is important that I question you. As much as you don't like"—his bemused gaze fastened on me—"or *pretend* not to enjoy being around me, you should get used to it. You'd be surprised how many women aren't bothered by it."

We drove up the driveway and into the garage of a tan midcentury modern home. I followed him up the stairs into an open and spacious floor plan. Recessed lighting gave off a hint of a glow. Floor-to-ceiling windows offered a panoramic view of the thick, lush forest that reminded me of the jungle. Large trees crowded the area and were just several feet from the house. A small opening in the bundle of poplars and oaks revealed carefully placed rocks that formed a waterfall that streamed into a pool.

I wasn't sure how long I was standing there admiring the breathtaking sight. But my attention was fixed when Gareth came up behind me, his chest against my back, so close I could feel the heat that radiated off it. His scent inundated the space that we shared. I had to remind myself over and over who he was, what he was, and where he worked. It became a mantra.

It didn't help. I turned, and we were close, just inches away from each other. Our eyes met and neither one of us made the effort to look away. All I had to do was lift my head and our lips would touch. Just as I was about to, he jerked his eyes from mine and looked at the yard. "You know you don't have to go out there to clean up, I have a shower here," he said and nudged me toward the right and guided me down the hall. We passed an office with a large desk similar to the one he had at the Guild. The built-in library was filled with leather-bound books, I assumed first or collector's editions, but I only had a chance to glance at them in passing. Surprisingly, the only thing that decorated the tan walls were windows. The home was fully furnished in various hues of deep brown and dark green with mahogany furniture, but with his walls he took a minimalistic approach. No pictures, just occasionally an oddly placed collection of metal art.

He led me to the bathroom. "You can just toss your clothes out here. There's a clean robe and t-shirt if you like."

I showered in what had to be the most luxurious bathroom I'd seen in my life. It should have been a quick shower, but it turned into nearly twenty minutes. My body ached, and the warm water felt good against my skin. By the time I was showered, I felt more human and less like shapeshifter fodder.

Walking down the hall toward the kitchen, where I heard Gareth, I fought the urge to snoop and only peeked into the rooms whose doors were open enough for me to glance in. He had a style, but I wasn't sure what you'd call it. Maybe expensive furniture–earth tone–leave me alone chic.

He stood at the kitchen sink, wistfully looking out of a large window into the jungle. He seemed like he'd rather be there than anywhere. And at that moment, I was fully aware what I was next to, the carnal primitive nature radiating off him. Man and beast forced into a symbiotic relationship. Before, I considered it a mutual acceptance and affinity, but at the moment, I wondered. He looked at the area with the appreciation and longing of a person seeing it for the first time. I saw the beauty, but didn't have the same love for forest and trees. The woods were where we hid, trying to throw off whatever Tracker was hunting us that day. They were where I learned fear, as I felt it rise and thrive in my parents. It was there I learned to fight, to use my magic that I was forbidden to use out in the world, where others could openly use theirs. It was in the woods, hiding, hoping not to be murdered, where my parents were given the daunting task of explaining to a five-year-old why she was reviled and would be hunted and hurt for the evils of others. Most of the time I pushed the memories back because they made my chest tight, captured my breath, and sullied my mood.

Gareth turned and his gaze slipped in my direction before he moved past me, his hand slipping over my back. I became more aware of how close he was, the warmth of his touch searing through the light fabric of the cotton robe. He'd showered, too; a hint of soap lingered on his skin and his white t-shirt was still slightly damp from where he hadn't dried completely. The soft fabric hugged his chest and abs.

Stop staring. I was giving myself the same command I'd given each time I went to Crimson.

He went to the fridge and pulled out two bottles of water and handed me one. Water was nice, but the type of day I'd had, something with a little more bite would have been better. Maybe he could tell it by the disappointed look on my face, or he felt that way, too, because he took a drink from his bottle and then pulled out two ales. He handed me one and placed another on the table and ducked back into the refrigerator. "Let's see what Leslie left for dinner."

Since I had no idea who Leslie was and why she was leaving food for him, I figured he was talking to himself. He pulled out several containers: macaroni and cheese—*yum,* gravy—*what's the gravy for?* And some type of chicken—Jerk —*I think.*

"Who's Leslie?"

He warmed the food in the microwave, then grabbed two plates, silverware, and a serving spoon. "She's the woman who helps out around the house, cooks, cleans, makes sure I don't burn it down." He grinned. "I'm not much of a cook."

"She takes care of you? So she's your nanny?" My lips quivered, making a poor attempt to stop the smile.

He let the slight roll over him and shrugged. "I call her the house manager, but I guess nanny is apropos, too. She's been with me since I was a child. I dare you to call her anything other than house manager." He took a long draw from his ale.

We sat at the kitchen table. Ignoring my frown of disgust, he poured gravy over his macaroni and cheese and then shoved a forkful in his mouth. When the frown wouldn't ease, he grabbed my fork, put some on it, and put it to my mouth. "Try it."

I shook my head and tightened my lips. I didn't come from the school of not knocking something until I've tried it.

And I didn't think gravy-covered macaroni was going to change me.

His lips pulled into a rigid line and mimicked mine in intensity. His defiant scowl remained. It was an odd time to have a battle of wills. I considered smacking his hand away, but I was sure that wasn't going to deter him. Crinkling my nose, I ate only half of what was on the fork. I had to win at least half the battle. He placed the fork on my plate. I ignored it in place of eating the jerk chicken, which may have easily been the best thing I'd ever tasted.

After taking a long drink from his ale, he asked, "How did you know that there was someone else performing magic?"

Ah, now I see why I have the ale. To weaken my inhibition. I was a woman who drank whisky straight, no chasers, and he would have to do better than apple juice with a kick.

"Asked and answered earlier," I pointed out.

He nodded slowly, still sipping on his drink. "Yes, I did. Why did you think that the magic went wrong? Or was there an inhibitor that was keeping her from getting to the memory? You automatically went to other magic. It's odd that you did."

He leaned into the table, his light blue eyes flooded with curiosity and that shapeshifter glint that was often a dead giveaway. "You are peculiar to me." He leaned back against his chair and crossed his arms.

"What's so peculiar about me?" I challenged.

In silence he continued to study me. I ignored him and concentrated on the food in front of me. After several more bites I took a drink from the ale, pushed the plate forward, and leaned against the table, watching him with the same intensity he had watched me with just seconds ago. I hated this game we had to play. I just wanted to find out who set me up, who was able to control vampires, and who had the type of magic that could control shapeshifters, because that was a very powerful and very dangerous person. I wasn't that danger, I didn't thirst for power. My magic wasn't catastrophic. I just wanted to be normal and not be hunted or have to worry about being killed if someone found out who I was.

I had to decide if I trusted Gareth with my secret. Did he have an oath he had to adhere to? I knew very little about him. Did he feel the same way others did? If I told him what I was, what would he do? When I looked at him this time, I studied him with a different interest, trying to interpret and understand how deep the predator lay. How intrinsic was the animal that he shared? How dedicated was he to holding up the laws of the Guild and the very covenant that bound humans and supernaturals together?

A wayward smile settled on his lips and enhanced his features, and it was hard to deny Gareth was a handsome man. Denying it didn't make it go away.

"I think humans can detect magic," he admitted. "I think the subtle nuances. It's that gut feeling that makes you believe someone is different, that ache inside of you. They might not be able to pinpoint it, but they know. When I walk in, I think people know I'm a shapeshifter or at the very least know that I am different."

Even if by chance you missed the ring around their pupils that was a couple of shades darker than their dominant eye color, I still thought detecting a shapeshifter was something that all humans could do. Whether shifters wanted to admit it or not, there was something about them. Like being near an animal. You know which one you can cuddle, hug, and play with and which one you need to stay away from.

"Necromancers are the only ones I know who can control vampires," I said. "And I don't know of anyone who can control shapeshifters."

129

"Animancer," he said. He seemed just as shocked by the word as it spilled from his lips.

"I've never heard of one. Do they really exist?"

"You know how I feel about things being so-called extinct. It is rarely true. Something that we tell ourselves to make us feel comfortable."

I shuddered under the intensity of his extended contemplation. Heat crept up my neck and cheek. *Fuck. Do you know?* My tongue slid across my lips, moistening them, and even though I took another drink from the bottle, my mouth was drier than it had ever been. He didn't do anything that led me to believe he did. Instead he got up and got another ale for both of us.

"Let's say we are dealing with one. Why would a necromancer and an animancer be working together? And are they the ones responsible for the last seven deaths?" He spoke so softly, I figured he was trying to work this out in his head. So many things didn't align. He frowned. "Unless"—he stopped, as if he didn't like what he was about to say—"unless, it's a higher-level mage. It's been rumored that some of them have necromancy abilities, similar to practicing dark arts. But I've never seen it or been able to confirm it. Knowing the mages as I do, I wouldn't put it past them to have started the rumor to vaunt about their power," he offered, displaying irritation similar to what he'd had with Jonathan at the Haven.

"We need to try to find one, and I'm sure that we'll find the other." Unless they weren't connected and were independent of each other. But I didn't believe in random events. A necromancer, an animancer, a missing Necro-spear, a dead witch, two dead: fae, mages, and shifters. They were all connected—not just to one another, but to me, too.

He stood. "It will probably be easier to find the necromancer or"—he scowled, and his voice dropped to a rumble

—"mage by using the controlled's sire. Tomorrow I'll go see Lucas."

Responding to my look of confusion, he said, "The vampire on the Magic Council."

Oh, the blond pervy one who wanted to know if the vampire looked horny.

CHAPTER 10

J wasn't sure if I was invited to go with Gareth to visit Lucas, but after I was dressed back in my clothes and in the car with him as we headed to my house, I invited myself by asking when he was going to pick me up to go see Lucas. I must have caught him off guard because there was an awkward pause. But after long consideration, he told me that he planned to go at eleven at night. Although vampires could walk in the daylight, they preferred night because it was when they were at their strongest. Weakened by the sunlight, they considered it an unnecessary hassle to go out in it.

"So you think that Lucas will know if there is a necromancer in town or a mage who has necromancer abilities?"

He considered it for a while as though he didn't want to give me misinformation, or was determining what information was appropriate for me to know. It was at that moment I knew that we weren't in a partnership. I was expected to disclose everything I knew; however, he was going to be selective about what he was willing to share. Which made me feel foolish for even considering, even in passing, telling him what I was. He was committed to the Guild, and his loyalties lay there, along with his commitment to protect and maintain the alliance that they had with the humans.

"He's responsible for siring most of the vampires in this area. He's linked to them and their progeny. When necessary a vampire can control and find his progeny. Hopefully, he will be able to direct us to the vampires who sired them and help me find out who is controlling the younger vampires. It's very hard for a necromancer to control an older vamp, so they will always go after the young ones. And vampires younger than a century old are still at the mercy of their sire."

When he drove up to my apartment, I told him I'd see him tomorrow, and once again there was an odd pregnant silence. I figured he was trying to decide if he was going to let me come with him. "If I'm with you, I'm probably going to stay out of trouble," I offered with a smile.

He chuckled. "I'll pick you up at eleven."

Savannah was on the couch watching TV when I came in, and she gave me the same assessing look that she'd been giving me ever since I got out of the Haven. I kept my arm turned palm down, hiding the fresh scarring. When I crossed my arms over my chest, it was totally concealed as I sat on the far end, trying to answer the laundry list of questions she had. I gave her a slight rundown of everything that had happened trying to give the amended "it wasn't that dangerous" version of it. No amount of editing could make letting a witch play inside my head, a magical attack, a fight with shapeshifters, and the possible discovery of a necromancer and animancer sound like just another day at the office.

"So you spent the day with Gareth?" Her interest was piqued and a wide grin took over her face. It was almost the same infatuated, whimsical look she had around vampires. I thought our last night at Crimson was enough to squelch her uncharacteristic and peculiar infatuation.

"Yeah, there was a bunch of other information before that, too," I said, narrowing my eyes at her in silent ridicule of her behavior. I lived with her and she still didn't get my glare of derision. Kalen could see it from across the room. It didn't really matter, though, because he always met it with a quelling look and a shrug of dismissal. Savannah was still smiling at me like a crush-struck tween. "He's very handsome."

"How do you know?" When she'd met him at the club she'd been drifting in and out too much to get a good look at him, and he'd left once he'd been informed she was doing well. All she knew of Gareth was that he was the guy who'd carried her out of a club; she wasn't in a position to identify him.

Her face streaked rose as she gave me a faint smile. "When they arrested you and I couldn't get in the Haven, I visited him several times. Ten times, to be exact. After I was escorted off the premises a couple of times, he agreed to meet with me. I guess he figured that was the only way to get me to stop."

I shrugged. "Did he threaten to have you arrested? Because that seems to be his thing."

"He didn't, but a couple of jerks at the Guild did. Along with the various threats of magic and spells they vowed they would use on me if I didn't go away. After my ninth visit, the woman at the front desk told me to have a seat, and she called him. An hour later, I met with him. For a man who was probably called out of bed to meet with me, he looked very good. Very. Good."

"So you're the reason they pulled me out of bed in the wee hours of the night to question me." I thought of Savannah storming down to the Guild in protest gear, engaging in her one-woman stand against the machine. "Well, you're lucky. He threatened to have me arrested when I refused to cooperate."

She dismissed it with a wave. "That's just misdirected courting."

"Hmm. So courting to you requires paperwork, bars, and possibly handcuffs?" I teased, raising an eyebrow. "I guess I need to watch you more closely, don't want you to get mixed up with the wrong crowd." She might have been swooning over him now, but if she got a look at my arm, she'd be swooning from afar, while interrogating him. I had edited the version enough that I didn't seem like I was in as much danger, which was why she'd drifted off into fangirl land, most of the conversation being redirected to focus on Gareth. Telling her he was a cave lion, would only have added to her fascination with him.

$\mathcal{I}$ was pretty sure Gareth hadn't planned on picking me up, but just when I was about to call him, he drove up. I had no idea where we were going and clearly I was underdressed for the occasion, in jeans, a fitted tank, and a jacket that moved easily with me and would not get in my way if necessary—my vampire slaying outfit. I'd had enough vampires taking plugs out of my arm that I didn't want to take a chance. He was dressed as he was the first time I'd seen him in his office. He had on black slacks and a button-down. The darker clothes made his eyes more brilliant. I didn't have to look back at Savannah to know she was looking at him. He was crush-worthy.

"Have a good night, *working*," she said from the door. I shot a glare at her over my shoulder, which she missed, or rather ignored.

"I didn't realize that I had to dress to question a vampire," I said as we made our way to the car. He stopped midstride and looked at me. His gaze roved, moving slowly over my face and stopping at my lips. He stepped closer. Then he continued to look, the curve of my neck, breast, and down and back.

"You look fine," he said in a low, even voice before making his way to the car.

We had driven for nearly a half an hour when we passed Crimson, the bar Savannah frequented, to pull up at another just five blocks away, where the sign was missing and a few people—vamps and a couple of humans—spilled out. I would have passed it and never thought twice about it if it weren't for the two men dressed in the same uniform: dark designer suits, burgundy shirt, one button opened, and faces diamond-cutting hard. The line was short; just a few people waited. One gentleman took their money, the other checked them.

I started for the back of the line when Gareth caught my wrist and led me toward the door. He was waved in, but one of the gentlemen stopped me.

"You'll need to remove the pins from her hair."

Damn. I'd pushed them in far enough that I thought they wouldn't be detected, and on the off chance we were stopped, I wore a cross around my neck, thinking that would be the only thing confiscated. They let me keep the cross but took the pins, which were nearly six inches long. When he examined them, taking in how sharp they were, he glared at me. My look of limpid-eyed innocence wasn't fooling anyone, but I tried. Wide-eyed and naïve, channeling a child-hood innocence that I wasn't sure I'd ever possessed. In the end, they even found and confiscated the knife I had fixed to my ankle.

The looks they shot in my direction were no longer signs of irritation—they were deadly. I stood between the two as they tested the boundaries of their power and dominance. Vicious and cool. I had the impression if Gareth wasn't standing there, they would have let me know their thoughts, and there didn't seem to be anything kind about them.

Gareth chuckled, a deep, melodious sound that mingled with the mesmeric music. The crowd moved seductively and sinuously to a provocative beat. Cool bodies moved around me; graceful people and their erotic movements commanded the room. Barely fettered lust cloaked every inch of the space. This wasn't like Crimson at all. It was darker and libidinous. A den of sin. People didn't dance here, they molded to each other in erotic motion that would extend to something off the dance floor. Vampires openly fed from people in the corner, and others walked around with glasses filled with sanguine liquid. It was the way I'd envisioned Crimson would be, but it had turned out to be just a simple club where the young vampires, taking their cue from television, were either flirty or broody. This was where the grown-ups played. As I walked through the unknown club, I quickly realized I was out of my league.

It was crowded, but not enough for the many hands that slid over me as though it couldn't be avoided. Each time I looked up to give whoever it was a dirty look, it was met with dark, alluring eyes and whispered invitations. Even with the short time I'd met Lucas, I could tell this seemed like a place he would hang out.

"What is the name of this place?" I asked Gareth after I'd received my seventh invite to have a "drink" and I was positive I was what they wanted to quench their thirst with. One quick look at humans being fed from and I was sure.

"Devour." His voice was laden with amusement. "Why, do you plan on coming back?"

"Not if I can help it." I wanted to make sure I had a name,

because if Savannah ever recommended this place, she was getting an emphatic no.

We reached the back of the club and then went up a flight of stairs. Again met by another suit-wearing guard, who checked us again. We opened the door to an apartment, and when he closed it, I forgot I was in the club. Silence.

A fully stocked bar on the right. And I had no idea why. A large kitchen with expensive stainless steel appliances, dark cabinets. The entire apartment had a theme of variations of black and gray. As we stepped farther into the dimly lit space, hints of light came from the sconces placed throughout the room. Gentle variations of black continued throughout the apartment, with the exception of the white sofa and chair. Quite odd for a person who frequently drank blood and surely had accidents.

"Olivia, I'm so happy to have you here." I heard Lucas's voice before he appeared from behind me and acted just like the rest of the touchy-feely vamps, his hand slinking over my back, hips, and down my arm before clasping my hand between his. Personal space was something he didn't seem to believe in or care to acknowledge. After several uncomfortable moments, I pulled my hands away.

"I never had the opportunity to apologize for the attack at my club. Did Savannah get my note and offer?"

She hadn't mentioned it, and I wondered why. Probably she knew if the offer was for her to come to this den of sin, I wasn't going to support it and would do what I could to stop it. "She hasn't mentioned it."

He frowned. "I sent it two days ago. Things have been quite hectic. Perhaps I will deliver it in person—"

"Give it to me, I'll make sure she gets it." I was sure that if Mr. All-American and Ginger had had her in full fangirl mode, this sinfully sexy man would have her quickly abandoning all logic.

"It was a check. I will deliver it again in person."

"When?"

"Perhaps tomorrow."

"What time?"

He simply smiled, casually amused, baring pearly whites and fangs. His features were as sharp and defined as those fangs he exposed. He walked over to the bar and poured himself a glass of something thick and red while I pretended it didn't look very close to blood. And then he poured two tumblers of vodka and handed them to us. I was about to decline mine when Gareth took it and took a small sip, and then smiled in appreciation. He took another sip; again he offered a look of appreciation. I took the glass, but just put it to my lips to taste. It was probably the best vodka I'd ever tasted, but unless it was in a Cosmo, I rarely drank it.

After taking a slow draw from his I decided to just call it really red wine, he asked, "Gar, my friend, what brings you here?" The way he said *friend* it was evident that they were far from it. Not enemies. Probably a mutual respect, but I was sure any animosity was deeply rooted in the fact they were both predators in their own rights. An existence independent of fae, witches, and mages. Immune to most magic, which afforded them certain advantages, they both had been the targets of it.

"I'm sure you are aware of the attacks that have taken place by your vampires, and you know they were being controlled by someone."

"I believe we have a necromancer among us," he said, clenching his teeth. He gripped the glass harder. I expected it to shatter, and it probably would have if he hadn't relaxed. The binding tension freed from his shoulders. Tilting his head in my direction, he studied me. A quaint smile flourished as he displayed an interest that was starting to make me feel uncomfortable. I crossed my arms, bringing my jacket around me more. He chuckled, a deep rolling sound, when I dropped his gaze and started to look around the room.

"I need the names of their sires; perhaps they can help me, or at least help me figure out when they lost control."

Lucas nodded, went to the antique writing desk, which seemed to be an anachronism in such a modern loft, and took a seat at it. It was an eloquent production as he used it to jot down the names. Dressed as he was in his dark green slacks, Italian shoes, and tailored hunter-green shirt, sitting at an aged desk composing a note didn't seem odd. I wondered how old he was and if at any time he missed things or got overwhelmed with changes that were so different from what he once knew.

As he handed the document to Gareth, he looked in my direction again, his smile faint, gentle, and chaste, different from the ones he'd given me before. "I, for one, hope it isn't a necromancer. I know they exist, but I would like to put our old ways behind us. Gareth, I hope that when you find this individual or individuals, you will allow me to speak to them prior to taking them to the Haven."

Gareth's lips drew together in a frown. "Will you be speaking to them on behalf of the Council?"

Lucas took another drink from his glass and turned his back to us, looking out the large window, his features locked in determination. "This person has made a mockery of my people. I've ensured that my progeny and theirs never be out of control. We are respected, something that we'd been denied for many centuries. Fear is fine, respect is better. How quickly the masses' minds have changed to considering us savages who lack control. So, no, I will not be speaking to him as a member of the Council, but as the Master of the city. Since those are the things you expect from me, I do believe it is in your best interest that you find him before I do."

"Lucas, just as I have a responsibility, so do you. As a member of the Council, you are bound by certain expectations and commitments."

He stood taller and sighed his discontent. "Oh yes, that Magic Council. How long have I been on it? Fifty? Sixty years?"

"Ten," Gareth offered.

"It does have a way of making time drag. Nothing interesting ever happened until"—he shifted his attention to me —"Ms. Michaels. Until your little incident, we met monthly, I guess to make sure we were all still alive. We all handle ourselves and our problems well. It is quite rare that we have a human in our court. I am curious how you ended up in it. There doesn't seem to be any steadfast criteria to the human justice system's decisions. Humans are quite fickle that way."

I almost laughed, both at his exasperated boredom with the Council and because he considered himself alive. He was a hot zombie—that's it. Instead of eating flesh he drank blood. And watching him consciously take inconsistent breaths, I assumed to make me feel more comfortable, was a freak show in itself.

"Gareth, the years I've dedicated of my time demonstrate my commitment to them. When I was forbidden to send a surrogate any longer, I gave them more than they deserved. My statement still stands."

"Lucas ..."

"Good night, Gareth." And he turned to focus on the exquisite view of the city that the picture window provided.

"No." Gareth's voice was hard with command. So much that Lucas turned from the captivating sights. "I understand your anger; I feel it, too. Yesterday, we were attacked by controlled shifters. But I can't allow you to behave like some vigilante. If you find him before I do, you will act on behalf of the Council and call me."

"My friend, that is where we part ways. Your dedication to the Council and your role as the head of the Guild are admirable, but your control is still limited when it comes to me. I am not your subordinate. I've existed before these rules and chain of commands that bind us today and, unfortunately, as I've conformed so much to the new world, that subjugation is beyond my ability. I will not interfere in any way, but if I find the culprit before you do, I will extend my own justice."

Lucas moved from the window, with the speed and grace I'd expected from a vampire. Although he'd moved in slow, measured steps before, giving the illusion of someone I shouldn't fear, I hadn't been fooled. The obsidian eyes watched me with such intensity it was as though we were the only ones in the room. His fingers lightly brushed against my skin as he took hold of the cross, letting it settle in the palm of his hand as he examined it. His smile gilded with amusement as he lifted his eyes to look at me. "I do hope that you and Savannah come to visit at a better time. I would very much like to entertain you without such other ugliness occupying my time." His voice dropped to a low, deep silkiness.

I smiled, and it was the fakest, most insincere one I could muster as I took a step back. The cross slipped out of his hand with ease, leaving him unaffected. A myth refuted with a simple touch.

"Of course. Sometime later will be great." My voice matched his, low and soft, my noncommittal acceptance as sincere as his offer. There was absolutely no way in hell I was planning to come back to visit him and let him *entertain*. That was clearly out of the question.

Whether he believed me or not, a self-assured confidence blossomed on his face as though he was aware of something I wasn't. Whether I intended for it to never happen, he intended otherwise.

An hour after Gareth had dropped me off, I still couldn't get all the things that were going on in my mind to settle. Someone was using magic that wasn't available to fae, witches, or mages. Once again I invited myself to go with Gareth, this time to meet the sire of the vampires who had attacked us at Crimson. He declined this time. Which was fine. There was more to this than the necromancer, and I wanted to find out.

I couldn't put the pieces together because none made sense. There was a vital part missing, but I didn't know what. My mind couldn't calm enough to fall asleep, which was why three hours after Gareth had taken me home, I was traipsing through the woods behind the trail I usually ran on, walking toward the cave pit I'd used when I'd performed magic on the Tracker. I dropped down in the darkness, flashlight under my neck. The small glint of light that the moon offered died out as I closed the cover.

In the cave, I burrowed the flashlight in the loose dirt. I needed to see if my suspicions were correct and a Legacy was near. That wouldn't necessarily explain the necromancy and the animancy—we had magic that affected both—but I wasn't sure if it was -mancy ability. But there could have been a spell. If it was a Legacy, it didn't explain the deaths and the stolen Necro-spear. I couldn't imagine one person was doing all of this. Whenever I moved somewhere, I often checked to see if there was a Legacy nearby, the way my parents taught me. It seemed like it would be a good thing for another one to be near us, but it wasn't. If it was one who wasn't doing a good job of hiding himself, then he could be outed to the Trackers and put us at risk of being discovered. So we were careful to make sure that there weren't any around because we were always careful—until we weren't. And when we weren't, my parents paid with their lives.

The cave was comforting to me, surrounded by the smell of the earth, closed away from the world. The confined space made me feel free, unrestricted by the laws and rules that bound me. Here I could practice my magic with freedom without the risk of being discovered. Nothing was ever foolproof, but the risk decreased significantly.

I checked the cover to make sure I had closed it all the way before I knelt down. I scooped loose grains of dirt into my hand and let them settle against my palm.

I didn't know why I always did it; I felt connected to it. Dirt was the foundation of it all, and in some way I—we—were the foundation of magic. Raw, undiluted power. I grabbed one of the twins out of the sheath and slipped it across my hand, and the blood that welled I used to draw a line across the ground. Then I whispered an incantation, performing one of the few spells my mother had taught me. The magic peaked; sparks of color, pink, blue, yellow, swirled around in a chaotic dance, bouncing independent of one another until they merged, forming a sheet that spread, darkening into a muted brown background. Light flowed over it, flicked along the long space. I knew it wasn't a lot of area, maybe a hundred-mile radius. A red spot shot off the sheet— my location. I waited as the colors washed over the map, bursts of other colors to indicate where magic was. It was a bursting firecracker of colors: fae, witches, mages. The Cleanse had killed so many, yet so many existed. I didn't agree with HF, but I could understand their concern. I was on the hunt for something else. I scanned the area looking for that red light. Another Legacy. My attention focused on a light that wavered. Hints of red twitched and then went out as fast as they would show. Long enough to be seen, but not enough for me to identify the location.

There was one in town. He might be hiding, but he wasn't innocent. I cursed under my breath. I had to find him. I ended the spell, watching as the colors pulled away as though they never existed and one by one disappeared into the ether.

Just as I stood, I heard light steps that echoed into the cavernous pit, so soft that if there were any noise at all, they would have been missed. I climbed up the ladder and pushed at the cover. It wouldn't budge. I was locked in. Holding a ball of magic in my hand, I hurled it at the cover; it slammed into it and withered into nothing as though it never existed. I didn't know what that was. A ward? If so, how did they arm it? I didn't have time to analyze it or try another spell. The steps were closer, just a few feet away.

I hopped down from the ladder and pulled the twins out of their sheath on my back and held them as the steps came closer. Out of the darkness of the pit, I heard one—no, two sets of steps approach me fast. Ginger and All-American emerged. Their dark eyes were empty and withdrawn as they had been before, piloted by an unknown force. With his dark eyes fixed on me as the target, All-American lunged. He moved slower than most vampires, jerky and stilted. Vampire slow was still human's full-out speed and even mine. It was obvious someone was controlling them, or perhaps their creator was trying to regain control. They halted, then lunged, erratic uncoordinated movements. I didn't want to kill them—they weren't acting on their own. I called the magic as I tried to push open the cover. Nothing. How powerful was this person to be able to control vampires while using defensive magic? I pumped magic through the sai; a spark, a light magical shove moved them back. Again, I blasted another shot at the lid. Nothing.

Ginger jumped at me, fangs bared as he soared. A

powerful front kick shoved him back a few feet. He attacked again; my elbow slammed into his nose, blood spurted. I side-kicked him and he went back again. All-American caught the handle of the sai on the bridge of his nose. He winced, and I lunged forward and planted one of the sai into his stomach, driving him back and pinning him to the crumbling rocks. He was secured against them. In pain. But that was fine. He'd get over it a lot faster than I would get over being dead. Ginger dodged my sai. I hated fighting with just one. Two was always better. Where one would fail, her twin was sure to succeed.

He struck me in the back, sending me facefirst into the wall. Pain seared through me, causing my eyes to water. The last thing I needed was to fight a vamp with compromised vision. I turned in time to see his hazy figure come at me. His hand swiped against me and I hit the ground with a thud. I rolled out of the way, just as his foot came down, barely missing me. Trying not to kill him lost priority. Stay alive—number-one goal.

I rolled over the ground and grabbed the sai that I'd lost when he hit me and thrust it into his leg. He growled as blood gushed and then I kicked at his groin. He folded in pain—vamp or not, a nut-kick is a woman's best friend. I pulled out the sai from his leg, drove it into his gut, and plunged him into the wall. The patter of more steps filled the dark space. *Fuck.*

I grabbed the knife from my ankle sheath, hoping that the pinned vamps with all their thrashing didn't manage to dislodge themselves. My vision was still blurry, but better. I couldn't wipe my eyes with my arms or clothes because there wasn't a spot that wasn't covered with dirt or blood. My heart raced: the steps were lighter, nimble—a fighter, not just some random vamp. Adrenaline still pumped in me, but I was starting to feel the ache, and waiting was killing me.

He burst through the darkness wearing a light suit similar to the one he'd worn earlier. Lucas. Brushing past at such speeds he seemed like a ghost who appeared next to me and disappeared before I could register its existence. Sword in hand, which I didn't notice on his approach. A quick strike and both vampires slumped down. He pulled out the sai and they dropped to the ground, and within seconds the bodies were ashes that blended with the dirt in the cave.

The sword gone, Lucas's hand was over my elbow as he guided me up the ladder. He punched at the cover; it didn't budge. After another failed attempt he dropped down, a bruising grip around my arm as he pulled me through the cave. It was happening too fast and I hated being manhandled by someone who had just killed two vamps whom I'd tried to save.

I stopped abruptly and yanked my arm from him, still feeling the warmth from his grip that would surely leave a bruise in the morning. "What the hell did you just do?"

"I took care of the problem." He took hold of my arm again. I couldn't see him—it was too dark and the flashlight was on the other side. I wasn't sure how far we'd walked because I was nearly running trying to keep up with Lucas. I wasn't positive that I wouldn't have fallen if he'd just dragged me along.

"They were being controlled by someone else," I hissed.

I couldn't see his face, but I could hear the cool drift in his voice. I was sure his face would be just as hard and impassive and was glad I didn't have to see it.

"Yes, this is the second time they've been used to do someone's bidding. Clearly their sire couldn't overpower him and that is a problem. They are the youngest, the weakest. Now they can no longer be used. Others will stand a better chance against being controlled." He sighed for my sake because he didn't need to breathe. I guessed it was important that he let me know he was at the end of his patience with being questioned. "Please, Olivia, I do loathe being underground." And with that he guided me along, although his grip loosened significantly once we neared another exit out of the cave.

He let me go first, and the moment I hit the surface I heard Gareth call my name. What was this, a repeat of just a few hours ago? I didn't feel like being questioned or making up a story to justify why I was in a cave at four o'clock in the morning.

Gareth gave me a once-over, frowned, and then directed his attention to Lucas.

"She was being attacked by my vampires, I took care of it." And with that he started toward a car several feet away. He looked back at me but I couldn't read the expression on his face. The piercing dark midnight eyes bored into me, making things uncomfortable. Did he sense magic, see what I'd done with it, or wonder why I kept getting attacked? *Welcome to the club, buddy, I'm wondering why I keep getting attacked, too.*

I could see the curiosity on Gareth's face. Lips that were usually pulled in a tight line were drawn back even tighter, eyes dulled with annoyance, and his arms were crossed over his chest.

"Why are you here?" I asked, letting irritation linger over my words. His predator's gaze widened just a smidge. *Yes, sir, I just pulled that.* I had to beat him to the questioning because I didn't have any answers that would make sense. And frankly I had better things to do than to think of something. Sodden from sweat and blood, my shirt clung to my body. Fatigue from the use of strong magic and fighting for my life had settled on me, and I needed to rest. My mind was racing with a multitude of thoughts, and exhaustion didn't allow the mental acuity I needed to sort it all out. Was it the Legacy behind the attacks and the murders? If so, why? And how did I stop him? Was he something different? To my knowledge, we only had animancy abilities, not necromancy. Magic wasn't immune to evolutionary changes; was this a new Legacy? It didn't matter if they were causing all of this chaos; I had to stop them before anyone else found them. I needed to stop them, because if they were caught by the Guild, our existence wouldn't just be the psychobabble of the Trackers; but absolute proof of our existence, and of the malice we were capable of. It would have been a ringing endorsement of why we were hunted and considered dead on sight. If self-preservation was selfish—so be it.

"Savannah said you were missing?"

Damn. Her mother-henning is going to ruin me.

"How did you know I was here?" I asked, startled.

"I tracked you here."

I assumed I knew what he was saying, but before I went into panic freak-out mode, I calmed myself down and asked, "How did you do that?"

"I know your scent. Once I know a person's scent I can track them anywhere in the city unless they mask it with magic."

Yeah, that's way up there with being one of the freakiest and scariest things I've learned about shifters. "And this can be done by all shifters?"

He nodded. "Some are better than others, but yes, it can be done. My senses are a little keener."

I was pretty sure this wasn't the right time to ask how to circumvent it, but I put it on my mental to-do list to find out.

I nodded as I started to back away, looking around the area, trying to get my bearings. I just wanted to get away from Gareth and the pit, which I probably couldn't use ever again.

I didn't know how far I was from my car. Lucas had been

pulling me so fast I had no idea how far we'd walked. Was it a few blocks or miles?

"It's on the other side about two miles away." The look of curiosity had heightened, marring his features. "I will take you home," he said as he started toward his car just a few feet away. The image of him driving with his head out the window, trying to catch my scent, brought a smile to my face.

He hadn't misspoken. Once we got in his car, he turned around and headed in the opposite direction of my car.

"Where are you taking me?"

"Home, like I said."

"I thought you misspoke. Take me to my car." I added a *please* because my words had lost all pleasantness and I sounded rude. I really needed a shower and a nap.

"No." He didn't mind sounding rude. His voice was hard and decisive. "Maybe if you don't have a car, then you'll stay out of trouble."

That was twice now that men had just started bossing me around, and it really left me unsettled. "I want you to take me to my car."

"Want's a funny thing, isn't it? I want you to tell me why you were in a cave at night fighting vampires and have the strong smell of magic coming off you. Yet I'm sure I'm not going to get my wants satisfied."

He sped down the street. I glanced at the speedometer—ninety. Jumping out of the car wasn't an option, and because there wasn't a lot of traffic, he barely stopped at signs and treated red lights like they were a suggestion. *Nice behavior, Mr. Head of the Guild.*

The car had barely come to a stop when I started to open the door, making sure not to give him an opportunity to question me. I needed time to come up with something.

"Ms. Michaels. I want you to shower, get a good night's

rest, and come up with a believable story about why you were out tonight and reek of magic. We can discuss it over brunch tomorrow at twelve."

I shrugged and sighed. "I was just out for a walk and saw the open pit and decided to explore." Oh, that was just an awful one. He was right, I did need some time to come up with something good.

The expression on his face was stern, all business. Usually there was a little hint of amusement, a smirk ready to emerge —but now there wasn't anything but pure stoicism. And he spoke with a grating deep voice. I was sure it was the one he used before someone got a really bad smackdown, whether physical or verbal. "You asked me not to threaten you with jail. Fine, I won't mention jail. What you are doing is obstruction. What do you think happens to people who do that?"

He'd finally lifted his eyes to meet mine. A balmy look of annoyance accompanied the assessment.

"Well, since we are being so polite to each other and using such beautiful insinuation. When someone behaves the way you are, I usually call them an ass. But I won't mention that because that's rude. What do you call people who ignore your request, leave you stranded without a car, and insinuate that they plan to put you in jail? *Donkey?* Or do you just go full throttle and call them *ass?*"

Those were the longest seconds, turning to minutes as I stood outside, the balmy wind bristling against my bare arms, the smell of vampire blood stronger than ever, and my shirt crusted with all the gore of the night. My pants weren't as bad, but the hardened blood made it more difficult to move.

He attempted a smile but had a hard time committing, and it was just a hard lift of one corner of his mouth. "Ms. Michaels, I will see you at twelve."

And before I could respond, he had sped down the street. Saying "No, you won't" really didn't have the same effect when snarling it at an empty parking space.

Savannah, eyes widened, opened the door before I could take out my key. She was dressed in her cult gear: Lululemon and gym shoes, ready to go pay tribute to the God of Fitness, which she did almost every morning at five. She stepped aside, her jaw moving slightly as though she was chewing on the words. Then her mouth opened and closed several times, lost for words until she finally settled on a frown.

"I'm glad you're okay. You want to talk about it?" she asked.

I shook my head. "Not now. You go pay tribute, and after I shower and get some sleep, I'll tell you everything. I promise."

It was a promise that I planned to keep. We'd been roommates for three years, and friends for four. She was my best friend, and I needed to unload the information that was weighing me down like bricks, and she needed to know because I had no idea how this was going to end. But I needed sleep. As restless as it might be, I had to try to force my mind to quiet for a while.

Surprisingly, I fell asleep, only to be awakened four hours later by Savannah knocking at the door. I also had five missed calls from Kalen. I didn't work on Saturdays typically, but sometimes he'd ask me to. I was hoping this wasn't one of those times. I just wanted to curl up in the bed and rest.

Savannah peeked her head in. "You need to come out. You really need to see this."

I rolled out of bed feeling every muscle aching, and I didn't want to check my body for bruising because I was sure a large portion of it was raspberry colored. On the way to the front room, I took a detour to the bathroom. I couldn't see anything if I didn't get the sleep out of my eyes. I didn't care how I looked, Savannah had seen worse.

Savannah stood in the living room a few feet from the front door. She jerked her head in the direction of the door. The Suits from Lucas's club stood there with a large basket with a card. Same style, different colors. This time they were dark brown—morning wear, I supposed. "Apparently, the only person they were given orders to give it to was you," Savannah said, irritated, standing on the other side of the room.

They handed me the basket; it was too large to hold and read the card at the same time, so I placed it on the floor, just glancing at the myriad of chocolate, fruit, cheese, and wine. It was a beautifully written script letter, and as I read it I was reminded of him sitting at the antique writing table, using an inkwell and pen to compose our list. I felt sure he'd composed the letter the same way.

Apologies for this morning. It was a situation that needed to be handled pragmatically. Albeit cruelly, it was a necessary evil. Please accept my gift and my invitation for dinner tonight as an apology.

How sweet, he killed two vampires whose lives I was trying to spare because they weren't acting on their own and he sent a basket and a letter. They might have deserved a seat at the douche table, but they didn't need to die. When I finished reading it, the Suits were still standing there.

Are they waiting for a tip? "I don't have any cash on me," I explained.

"No. We were given instruction to get a time."

"Oh. I'm not having dinner with Lucas," I said. "Tell him thanks for the offer, but I'll pass."

"That wasn't an option, Ms. Michaels."

"Call me Levy, and please tell your employer that's the

option I have chosen."

They didn't budge. They were built like walls so I was sure a gentle nudge wasn't going to help, either.

"We were instructed not to leave until you agreed to a time."

Nice, a pushy vampire, who wants to eat with me. I just don't need this.

"Call Lucas, please, I would like to speak to him."

They looked at each other, apprehensive, and eventually one of them took out his phone, pressed a button, and handed it to me.

"Ms. Michaels," he said, my name rolling off his tongue as though he were reciting a sonnet. His voice was as light and wispy as it had been the night at the club. Before I could say anything, he added, "I was expecting your call."

I was curious how he knew it was me, but not enough to ask. "I can't have dinner with you tonight."

"What night would be good for you?"

Ain't-going-to-happen day at seven never o'clock.

I sighed into the phone. "I don't want to have dinner with you," I finally said. "So will you send your Suits away?"

"Suits?" he repeated with a chuckle. "I must admit this is the first time I've ever been turned down." I was pretty sure there wasn't a bigger truth.

"Well, thank you for allowing me to be your first. I hope it was as good for you as it was for me," I said in a light, cloying tone. "Seriously, thank you for the offer, but no thanks. The Suits will be bringing back the basket as well." And I disconnected. Lucas seemed to require very little to be encouraged. Accepting a gift from him was going to do just that.

I waited, but the Suits didn't move, and I doubted that they would have if it weren't for a call from Lucas. After it, they grabbed the basket, moving almost in unison, turned, and left.

"You must have had a heck of a morning," Savannah said from her seat on the couch, moving to the end to give me room. She seemed ready to hold me to my promise.

I grabbed a large cup of coffee and took a seat next to her as she waited patiently for me to speak. One sip of coffee became half of the cup while I wished for something a little stronger. Taking another long sip, I looked for the fortitude to keep from reneging on my promise.

"What do you know about the Cleanse?" I finally asked after a long, uncomfortable silence.

She looked confused by the question and took a moment before she answered. "Pretty much what everyone does. Demigod types with helluva magic who decided they wanted to be the only supernaturals who existed." She displayed the same abhorrence at the memory as someone would discussing a war that was started by greed and the thirst for power. "They stayed hidden behind a veil that was secured by a ward while the world crumbled at their feet. I assume when the damage was done and most of the population was decimated, they would have gotten off their self-important asses to collect the rest as slaves. Well, that's what I believe. In school they tell a nicer version. I guess not to warn us off the supernaturals. You know that whole 'not everyone is bad' and 'everyone deserves a gold star' BS."

This was going to be harder than I thought, and at that moment, I decided I couldn't tell her. I took another drink and let her continue, because she looked like she was revving up for another long spiel.

"Some good came from it. The supernaturals came out. We formed an alliance with the supernaturals, and where would we be without the witches and their wonderful shops, and let's not forget, the *herba terrae*?" She grinned, but then her look became dour, sad. A memory that may not have been her own, but spun from generation to generation of the retelling of the same story, bloviated and changed for effect.

"I lost family in it. I think a lot of people did. It's sad that —what was it? Eighty-nine people?—could cause such havoc that the world changed. I was told there was a small resistance that tried to stop it but failed. Where they failed, high mages were able to tear down the ward and an army who blasted the city behind it succeeded."

The sorrow in her voice was a reminder of why I wanted to tell her. Even through the anger of her loss, the travesty of the situation, and the wrongdoing—she had compassion.

"There was a small resistance of thirty-six, who failed and were able to get out before everything happened. My parents were two of them."

When understanding settled over what I had just said, her mouth dropped. She quickly snapped it shut and managed an "oh."

With a wry smile, in a low voice I admitted something I had never said out loud. "I'm a Legacy."

She nodded slowly, her mouth twisted to the side as she thought for a while. "Why were you covered in blood last night? You weren't doing some weird freaking spell thing? Because I'm okay with the Legacy thing, but the other stuff is a no-no."

I laughed, and with all the horrible things going on, that was one thing that was lifted. The burden of carrying it around was heavier than I thought, because I felt like I was floating. And then I told her everything from the Haven, my meeting with Clive, all the things he'd said, what I had discovered in the cave, and even the Trackers who had killed my parents and the ones who'd found me. It was then that she seemed to understand the severity of the consequences behind my secret. I didn't need her to swear to secrecy, I knew she would never tell anyone.

"Are you sure it was a Legacy who was blocking your spell?" she asked. "It flickered, could it be that they were ..." She stopped. "Maybe a Tracker or someone ..." She didn't finish; a despondent look replaced her words. I knew what she was thinking, and it was aptly displayed on her face—that flicker could be me.

"Possibly. I am just trying to figure things out. Was it coincidental that I ended up in the park that night? Is someone trying to set me up? Who is it and how are they able to control both shifters and vampires? What is the reason behind it?" Speaking of shifters, I looked at the clock: it was eleven thirty. "I'm supposed to meet Gareth for brunch."

"I'll call him and tell him you're sick or something. You don't look too good to me, you could use a couple extra hours of sleep. You go to sleep and I'll handle everything. And when you get up, we'll figure this out."

I wasn't sure if she was going to be able to handle Gareth —I didn't think he was the type to be handled—but I was cautiously optimistic. But things did seem a lot brighter with another set of eyes looking at the problem—someone I didn't fear could hurt me or bring an army against me.

I closed my eyes, but a nap wasn't going to happen anyway because I was thinking about what Savannah had suggested. What if the flicker was just a dying Legacy? *Dammit.*

When Savannah knocked on my door a little before twelve, I rolled over and said to the closed door, "I guess you weren't able to handle it. I'm sorry you had to deal with the shifter with an attitude. He's kind of an ass. You should have just told him to bugger off."

"Why don't you come out here and tell him yourself?" said Gareth's deep, coarse voice that held just a tinge of

158

humor. He was a shifter with an attitude and a warped sense of humor.

"Fine." I hopped off the bed, yanked open the door, and found Gareth resting against the wall, sporting a devilish smirk and holding his Guild badge and a set of handcuffs. "You have a choice, Ms. Michaels. We can talk at the station, at the Haven, or at a nice brunch. I'm fine either way."

Working with Kalen had taught me the art of compromise, because I didn't think I'd met anyone more stubborn, self-centered and arrogant than him—until now.

As I turned around to go get dressed, the things I mumbled under my breath surely should have wiped that smile off his face. I looked over my shoulder. It was still there. He was definitely a smug one.

There wasn't any way I was going to eat a cheeseburger and fries, Belgian waffles, wings, a grilled chicken salad, chocolate cake, and cherry tart, but I ordered it anyway. My passive act of aggression toward Gareth didn't work. The condescending look of indifference had become a fixture on his face and removing it was going to be an ongoing goal.

Once the food was ordered, he sat back and cocked his head. "This morning. Tell me about it."

I shrugged and kept my voice devoid of any emotion. "I came home. I couldn't sleep, so I went for a jog on my usual trail. It's not unusual for me to do it."

"You jog often in the dark?" Doubt vibrated in his voice and in the twisted corners of his lips.

"Not often. Just when I can't sleep."

"So you went for a jog, and what, fell in the cave?"

Oh, that's good, I wish I'd thought of that one. "No, I saw it

159

open and was curious." I hated lying. I did. But I didn't have a lot of choices.

"So in the middle of the night, you decided to explore a cave. It's just coincidental and advantageous that you had tools to open the cover, a flashlight, and your sai with you," he offered in a breezy tone.

"I take the twins almost everywhere."

The food had come, and instead of focusing on his cool glare of disbelief, I focused on eating the waffles and asked for the rest to be put in to-go containers. I could feel his stony glare home in on me. His fingers moved casually over the edge of his glass as he spoke. His tone was low and detached.

"The funny thing about lying, the mouth can tell as many of them as you want, but the body will always be honest. Increased heart rates and respiratory sounds. Blinks that either increase or decrease, and the cadence of the voice will always change when a person lies. Did you know that, Levy?"

"Yes. I also realize that a person's heart rate might increase because they are being interrogated by a person who's threatened more than once to throw them in jail. The cadence in their voice might have changed because each time they speak, they're trying to refrain from asking said Guild Commander why he is such an arrogant, narcissistic, smug"—I stopped short, no need to be vulgar—"donkey. I'm blinking more or less because I'm tired, because I've only had a few hours of sleep the whole week after being attacked by controlled shifters and vampires, Commander."

If that didn't wipe the smug off, nothing would. It didn't, but the corners of his lips curled slightly. He was handsome. The relentless wayward smile, smirk, or whatever looked good on him. I realized I was staring at him, and not out of contempt. I jerked my gaze away and focused on the waffles, which were delicious even lukewarm.

"Look, Gareth, I want to find out who's responsible for this just as much as you do. Interrogating me, calling me a liar, trying to poke holes in any story I tell you isn't going to help things. Maybe you should start trying to find the person who's controlling the shapeshifters and the vampires." I didn't want to tell him that there might be a chance of a Legacy being involved. Savannah had a point: the flicker could have meant they were dead, but also could mean that they were trying to stay hidden. The problem with pointing out that there was one Legacy was that it could cause him to wonder if there were more. I didn't want him questioning that.

"Why don't you tell me what happened with you and Lucas in the cave?"

I nodded and proceeded to tell him what happened, leaving out the parts about me using magic to stop them and trying to find out if there was a Legacy nearby. Whether I was right or wrong, either way it was a bad situation.

"Are you okay with letting Blu try to retrieve the memory, again?"

This again? But I needed to; even if all we had was a face, it would lead us somewhere. I nodded, and moments later he sent out a text and she responded, telling us she'd meet us at the house. I had two bags of food to carry out that Gareth grabbed, but not before he made an unappreciated snarky remark. Just as I opened the door, I saw the familiar figure across the street. He sat outside on the patio across from the restaurant where we had had brunch. He shifted his attention between Gareth and me. Under his intense scrutiny I recounted his words about HF and change coming and that things were in the works. It was just another thing on my list that could be linked. As much as I dreaded it, I needed my memory back.

Blu met us at the door, and if it were possible, I thought her hair must have expanded. A coarse waterfall emerged from her head, the blue tips a couple of shades lighter than the off-the-shoulder long Bohemian dress that swayed gently as she walked along, a cluster of bangle bracelets around her wrist. The same friendly smile welcomed us into the home. This time she didn't bother to offer me *herba terrae*. Without wasting precious time, she had me seated in the same position as the other day. The mark on my forehead tingled, and warmth flitted and slowly enveloped my body.

"I want you to relax," Blu said in a mellow low, raspy voice, but it was hard to do when she couldn't. I could feel the tension. Fear. And it was hard to hide it.

Gareth kept his eyes on her, and if I could hear it, he could, too. I was sure he could sense it, hear it in her vitals, and probably even smell it.

I inhaled the aromatic scents of the room, allowing them to relax me even more, accepting the journey I needed to take to get the answers we needed.

The club. I remembered the sounds of music that consumed the room, bodies moving, the strong smell of liquor and the potent fragrance of blood off the vampires that drifted throughout the crowded space. I recalled the people, conversations, and then the attack.

I tried to keep my eyes closed, but I could hear Blu's labored breathing as she struggled for every one she took. My eyes snapped open to find her wide-eyed, her palms turned up. Magic pulsed off her like a brush fire. Her lips moved fervently, reciting invocations, before her body became rigid. Magic saturated the air, not just hers. Familiar magic, but different from Blu's, Kalen's, and even the one I'd felt the last time. Blu howled in pain and was slammed back so hard against the wall, plaster crumbled around her as she slumped to the floor. Her limp body collapsed. Her breaths came in short bursts.

Another gust of magic shot through the air and pounded into her motionless body. I grabbed the knife out of my ankle sheath and darted out the door. I wished I had the twins, but just as with a sword, it was really hard walking down Main Street with them without risking getting odd stares and possibly an unrequested police escort to wherever you were going. If I wanted to stop the magic being used against Blu's, I had to stop it at the source. Outside, I let the magic wash over me, assessed the rhythm of it and the subtle variations that made it uniquely the practitioner's. Supernaturals knew that all magic's source could be identified once they knew the owner. Like every musician has a sound that makes their music uniquely theirs, so does a magic user have a magic that is only theirs. I'd felt this brand of magic at the Haven, when Jonathan sent an explosion of it into me.

Where are you, bastard?

Curses and spells could be done from a distance, but they were much stronger the closer the practitioner was to the target. But you had to be close to perform defensive and offensive magic. You couldn't toss someone across the room if you were hundreds of feet away.

Knife in hand, I went around the house, following the motes that drenched the air from used magic. I darted around the large trees that crowded the area. The magic aura became too light to trace. He was gone or had stopped using it. In a thicket in the forest, I scanned the area, listening for sounds and trying to distinguish them from those of nature. I heard a branch break off to my right, and light footsteps. I ran, catching the shadowy figure as he moved deeper into the forest. It wasn't Jonathan—this guy was several inches taller with lighter brown hair. The closer I got, I could sense the silhouette of magic that seemed to follow him. Strong but familiar. He didn't walk as much as he seemed to glide with the grace and agility of a vampire.

When I was just inches from him, he whipped around. Broad, sculpted features and a hook nose. Supple lips formed a sharp straight line. The magic was familiar because it was the one I felt when Blu was attacked, and the same magic had been present when the shifters attacked us. He wasn't fae, or mage. Legacy? No, this wasn't my magic—it was different, purer than pure. It was too much, a potent dose that was too much to take. An overwhelming surge of magic that needed to be diluted. It needed to mix with something that a person could take and actually survive. Who could go up against him and stand a chance? I stood, staring at someone who made what I was pale in comparison. His eyes flashed and my body was seized, forced still. He glided toward me in silence, each step reminding me less of a vampire and more of a predator in the jungle, ready to attack.

I hated the silence, I felt submerged in it as though the world stopped, and everything around me seemed so small. Transfixed by his eyes, I was unable to pull away. He stepped closer, his lips barely moved, but I could feel magic pouring over me, clouding my mind, plucking at my thoughts. He was trying to pull something out, a memory—this memory. The memory of him.

My head hurt from the sudden attack of magic. I recalled every session with my mother when she'd taught me reversal spells, some of the few I had been allowed to learn. I went for the strongest. I was always taught when performing spells that specificity was important. I didn't have time to be specific; I pushed, magic full force. Harder, stronger than anything I'd used in my life. My binding broke free, but not without consequences. My skin felt excoriated, as though I had physically ripped myself out of the binding. He shuddered, the first emotion he'd shown. He looked around. I heard it, too—footsteps. Then Gareth called my name. He tried again to pull the memory, a flick of his hand tossing me back against a tree. My head slammed into it. Dizzy. The buzz of his magic overtaking me. Pulling. Yanking. Attacking. If he was a Legacy … he was a Legacy 2.0. Upgraded to dangerous level.

Gritting my teeth, I pushed back. He stumbled back. A smile of wry appreciation and interest cloaked his features. Pulling in the magic, forming a massive ball of it, I thrust it out. He crashed back. Gareth's voice rang in the air. The man was on his feet again. Pushing me back against the tree. Another hard shove; I saw color, my head began to swim, and more colors coursed over my eyes in vibrant sparks. When he tried it again, I blocked it. I needed the memory. I needed to remember him.

More magic—hard magic—blasted from me. He grunted; I'd done damage, but I couldn't see how much. I had a hard time focusing. It took me a moment. I stood, head cloudy, but I wasn't going to let him get away. I stumbled after him, vision blurry. I made out the faint smile as the air opened up and he slipped through. No. I must have been more injured than I thought. He didn't just open up the air and walk through it. A veil. He slipped through a veil.

I wanted to clear my thoughts, shake my head, but it hurt too much to do so.

"Levy, are you okay?"

I spoke, and I didn't recognize the sound of my own voice. Exhausted from using magic that I hadn't let free in years. My body ached like I'd worked it too hard. My head throbbed from breaking a spell and being pounded into a tree. "How's Blu?"

"She's fine—a lot better than you seem to be. You don't look so good."

"I'm fine." *I said that out loud, right?*

I cradled the blanket closer to me, shrugging at the relentless tapping on my shoulder, which was becoming annoyingly more frequent. Then there was a light shake. Again I tried to shrug off their touch.

"Levy, sit up!" Gareth's voice was deep and commanding. Stern enough to open my eyes, even if it was just to give him a dirty look.

"Why are you yelling at me?"

"Sorry, I have to wake you up every two hours. If not, you're going back to the Isles."

I rolled over and sat up on the side of the bed. "Back?"

"Yeah, you kept saying you were okay, but you passed out right before telling me not to take you to the hospital. So I made a compromise. I took you there, had you checked out, and now you're here."

I looked around the large, simple room. Dark furniture: dresser and armoire. Bare cream-colored walls. Curtains, covering a large ceiling-to-floor window, drapes drawn, making the room exceptionally dark. If it weren't for the light spilling in from the hallway and the gentle glow of a small cylinder light next to me, the room would have been pitch-black.

"Okay, well, I'm awake. You can take me home."

An amused laugh filled the room. The gentle illumination cast little flecks of light over his eyes, just enough to make them glint with his chuckle. "That's not part of the deal."

"You made a deal with a barely conscious person? Pretty shady."

He shrugged, the smile still settled on his face, lips kinked. "Fine, the Haven it is."

I glared at him. My head was aching so much that a good eye roll was out of the question.

"Get some sleep, aspirins are on the nightstand. You've been okayed to take them. The sandwich is for you if you want it." And then he closed the door. It was nearly dark. I touched the metal of the small cylinder lamp and it brightened and offered more light. I liked to see what I was eating. I took a bite out of it. It was hard to be mad at him while stuffing my face with a turkey sandwich on a croissant with pepper jack cheese and a delicious spread that brought it together beautifully. His nanny, lady of the house, house manager, or whatever title he gave her had just been given the title of world's best sandwich artist. And when I noticed the homemade cookies on the plate next to it, she had been upgraded to new friend.

When I awoke for the second time, I had no idea how long I'd been asleep. The room was totally dark; someone had turned off the small nightlight. I tapped it once and enough light came off it for me to find my phone on the table. Only one text from Savannah, which meant she must have spoken to Gareth.

I sat up for a moment, letting the images of today that had been dormant come alive. Fear coursed through me as I remembered the strength of his magic, potent and familiar. Magic sheathing my skin to remove my memories again. A spell that could remove my memories of his face so I couldn't tell anyone. He was familiar, but not a Legacy. There was something distinctly different. Was he afraid the way I was in the cave and the very first time I'd seen a Tracker? Did the memories of watching his family murdered by one cause him to react out of self-preservation? I couldn't believe that I was torn by this innate odd alliance to a person whom I'd met for mere moments when he had attacked me. I closed my eyes, and all the thoughts and memories melded together. I tried to make sense of it.

It was obviously the man from the woods who took my

167

memories; but why? Was it to protect me? He could have killed me that night. Did I see something and he feared it would put me in danger? Jonathan, what was his role? There were too many unknowns and variables that made things too difficult to figure out.

After sitting up, I went back to bed. Gareth came in again to wake me up. He asked me a few questions and then let me go back to sleep. It was a little after ten at night when I finally felt rested enough to get up. Moving to the edge of the bed, I expected a headache, but luckily it was gone, although there was still soreness. I had definitely hit a tree, and I wasn't totally convinced a car hadn't rammed into me. Stretching didn't help, either, but it seemed to make the bound muscles loosen enough for me to move better.

Silence bothered me. Often it meant danger. Predators and Trackers moved in silence. I called Gareth's name as I made my way through the house; only a light at the end of the hallway was on, but it was enough to illuminate the long path. I'd finished the water in my room, and even while half asleep, I'd burned through the sandwich and cookies. I went to the kitchen to get some food but quickly became distracted by the view outside—the forest that stretched so far and tall that I could just see the top of the neighboring home in the distance. Gareth came out from it, a hint of moonlight offering enough light for me to distinguish him as he emerged naked before stepping into a pair of jeans. Once again, I had seen his exposed body. I looked too long, focusing on his chest, broad and defined, his strong features and captivating eyes. I was disappointed in myself for staring. I started to look away, but not before he caught me.

A hint of a smile graced his supple lips and remained as he approached the house, holding eye contact the whole time. I found it hard to look away. He was quiet as he entered the house and neared me, slow movements as though he was approaching cowering prey. I didn't cower, but maybe I should have, just so I'd have had a distraction. I needed a distraction. And when he reached out to touch me, I jerked back like he was a flame and I was trying to move out of danger. Smiling, he ran his hand over the back of my head, where I assumed he figured I'd hit it. The hint of oak drifted off him and I inhaled, breathing him in.

"No lumps. It *is* as hard as I suspected."

"Is that how you treat a guest in your home? Real nice, Mr. Gareth."

He didn't move. Instead he remained close, holding my gaze in the same manner he had walking to the house. And I found myself just as entranced by it. *Look away.* Savannah was getting an apology for being vamp fangirl, because I had a feeling I was falling into one of my shifter fangirl moments. I was aware of what was happening, an attraction that was probably more primal than anything. It wasn't real. It was just his presence speaking to a carnal part of me—or that's what I was trying to convince myself of. Whether it was the truth or not, I needed to ignore it.

"How do you feel?"

"Fine. No headaches. Nothing. Back to my old self." But was I? My *old self* was able to overlook how handsome Gareth was. My *old self* didn't fixate on his lips and wonder what it felt like to kiss them. My *old self* didn't let inappropriate thoughts pop in my head and stay.

His lips pressed lightly against mine. Then again, a little more commanding, harder. Responding, I moved closer, digging my fingers into the skin of his waist. His body pressed next to mine; one hand wrapped around my waist, the other threaded through my hair, pulling me closer to him. He abruptly pulled away.

"Now that's out of the way, maybe you can concentrate." He stepped back and leaned against the counter, wearing the smuggest smirk of all smug smirks.

This is why I haven't been enthralled by him—haughty, smug, narcissistic. How did I let that escape me, even for a moment?

"What?"

"You were staring at my lips, I'm sure wondering what they felt like. Now you know."

I was glad it didn't hurt to roll my eyes now because I did just that, and hard.

"Do you need another, or will that do? I can give you another."

I tossed a cold look in his direction that only encouraged him. "I'm fine."

"What happened today?" he asked, his voice a little rougher, deeper than usual. He held my gaze for a moment, then directed his attention past me. It kept drifting back to me and then to my lips before he moved it away. Seemed like Gareth needed to get it out of the way more than I did.

"Some jackass gave me a magical TKO."

"What did he look like?"

"Thin—very. Tall, a little over six feet. Brown hair, sharp features, cold, empty gray eyes. I've never seen him before. Dressed odd, long coat, embellished. Slacks and a white shirt. I don't know if he was the one who stole my memory before, but he tried to steal it then. I—" I stopped abruptly. I'd nearly told him everything. Including how I fought him off.

"You what? What did you do?"

"I fought him off." So what that I left off the part about doing it with magic?

"Did you see Jonathan?" he asked. "I could smell him close to the house."

"No." My words were clipped and I forced myself to say just that, although I'd almost said that I had sensed his magic.

I was getting careless around Gareth, dropping my guard. He was one of the last people I needed to drop my guard with.

"You don't think he's involved in any of this?" I asked.

I expected an emphatic denial; after all, he was on the Magic Council. It wasn't as though they were infallible, but status and honor went with the position and I can't imagine that there were many things that would cause them to sully the reputation of the Council or jeopardize their position on it. But obviously Gareth didn't feel that way based on the long moments of deliberation.

"I don't know," he finally admitted, scrubbing his fingers over his face, then through his hair. I jerked my eyes away from him and settled them on the beautiful view outside. The waterfall, its gentle splashes, and the shimmer of the moon that reflected on it were soothing. "I've called him several times without a response. Which is just as well, I prefer to question people in person."

I knew it was so that he could ascertain if the truth was being told or not. He looked over at his phone, which had started to vibrate. I assumed it was Jonathan, finally returning his call. He glowered and looked back at me. "Tell Savannah I will not hesitate to block her number. Does she realize that I'm not your court-appointed guardian?"

I shrugged a response, trying hard to ignore his lips that were pressed against mine just minutes ago. *Focus on the issue*, I scolded myself, but I had a hard time redirecting. I was embarrassed that he had affected me that way.

He pushed up from the counter and turned, his body sidled in so close that I could feel the ridges of his abdomen. "I'd invite you to stay the night, but I don't think I care to have to deal with Savannah's excessive calls." And he disappeared down the hall. He returned with a shirt, and we headed to the car.

CHAPTER 12

*S*avannah held the blade with the skill of someone who actually knew what she was doing with it. But she stayed close as we entered the dense woods near the home Blu used to perform magic. Each one of her steps were measured and slow.

"Why don't we call Gareth and get backup?"

"Because I don't work for the Guild, and I don't think I can call for backup." My voice matched hers in a gentle low cadence. I would have loved to go at this alone, but the moment I told her my plans to find the man who'd tried to steal my memory, she wasn't having it. I realized that her siblings probably chose universities out of the city to get away from the overbearing big sister. I was just six months younger and I was suffocating under her "help."

"Just to make sure I have this straight: you want to go into the spooky forest alone, with me as backup, so you can find a magical veil and a man who you said, and I quote, 'gave me a magical ass kicking'?"

I stopped, grinning and baring all my teeth. "Yeah, that sounds about right."

She pulled out her phone and I knew who she was about to call. "Savannah," I hissed through clenched teeth.

Startled with my anger, she jerked. And as she asserted herself, she placed her hand on her hips. It was lecture time. "He has a seat on the Magical Council and is head of the Supernatural Guild, why wouldn't you call him?"

I sighed, heavy and deep. "For those very reasons." I stepped closer; even in the empty woods I didn't feel safe saying it out loud. "You know what I am. The less time I'm around him the better."

"He seems okay."

"Are you willing to bet my life on it?" I asked gravely. Then I started to back away. "At the end of the day he has a job to do. He's threatened to put me in the Haven for obstruction, what do you think he'll do if he finds that out?" I started walking again. "And all the kissing in the world isn't going to keep him from doing his job."

"Kissing? Who … hey, you're holding out on me." She rushed forward and fell in step with me.

I forgot I left that part out of my retelling of the story. It was silly. "I'll tell you later," I said, and as I kept walking I felt her glare on me. I ignored the smart remark she grumbled as we advanced farther into the forest. I slowed when things started to look familiar and the magic increased. It caressed me at first, a familiar touch, but as I got closer, it clouded the air, becoming thicker, pricking at my skin. The unique feel and smell of it called to me. So close to mine, yet so very different. If it were described as colors it would be eggshell and white. Very subtle, but it was there, and only when a swatch of each color was put together could you tell the difference.

My magic was next to it, simultaneously taking up the same frequency, almost duplicate. I came to an abrupt stop, feeling the powerful roil of it.

Savannah stopped, close. Too close. She was scared. The guilt burned deep and gnawed at me. I was glad I'd told her what I was. She needed to know. But on some level I had put her in danger and I hated that.

"Savannah, I need you to step back. I am going to attempt to open the veil. You stay here, away from it. In fact, step about ten more feet back." She did and looked relieved to have as much distance away from magic as she could.

Running my hand along the seams of the invisible wall, I felt for a weakness. A part where I could break it easier. I found it. I pressed my hands against it and forced power, causing it to waver but not open. Again, another charge of magic, and it dipped in farther. Just as I was about to give it another thrash, I was yanked in and spat out on the other side. Tumbling in, I came to my feet, sai in hand, just in time to catch the sword in the moto of one sai. I stabbed with the other; Magic Stranger shifted to the side and I missed. I swiped his foot, he crumpled to the ground, and his sword slipped from the sai, but fell a few feet from him. He retrieved it and flipped into standing, his slim body agile as he thrust forward. He missed. I spun around. A sai caught him this time in the side and then I slid it across his abdomen. He stumbled back and made a face of surprise as blood spread from the cut and stained his pastel-colored shirt. He stepped back, watching me as his weapon rested at his side.

I rested mine, too, but maintained a defensive stance, ready to engage if necessary. He moved his hand over the wound; it closed and the blood slowly disappeared. He smiled and grabbed his sword and charged me with a forward strike. I shifted and cracked the butt end of my sai into his back. And I gave him a positional advantage: he looped his arm around my hip and tossed me to the ground, causing me to lose one sai. It landed near his feet and he grabbed it. "To die by your own weapon is by far the worst death."

Jumping to my feet, I used the one sai to catch the sword coming in my direction, but he jammed the other sai toward me and then wailed in pain, dropping it next to me. "It's enchanted. I have no fear of dying by my own weapon." And I sent a thank-you to my mother. She'd taught me to fight with it. And feeling the same abhorrence about the worst death being one by one's own weapons, she'd made sure I never would.

He stayed kneeling. If I didn't know any better I would have thought he was bowing to me. "A warrior and Legacy. We will need more like you," he admitted, his voice now smooth, without the rough edge it had had when he'd taunted me about dying by my weapon.

"You're one, too."

"Yes and no."

"It can't be yes and no. It's either one or the other."

"Then yes," he said with a coy smile.

He tried to relax as he did, and it didn't seem like he was going to attack again. I looked at the stretch of land that nearly mirrored the forest that I had just left, but farther away there were buildings—not many, three in sight—but there weren't any people.

"You have your own world. That must be a serious ego boost."

The musical sound of his laughter filled the air. I would have thought it was a lovely sound if it were not mere minutes ago that he'd tried to cut me up into bite-size pieces.

He stood straighter, dressed as he was before in a long coat, a light-colored shirt, and dark pants. He was regal in appearance but fought far less delicately than he looked.

"Who plans to live here?"

"Our allies and others who will be our servants."

"And which do you consider me?"

"You are a Legacy, one of us."

"Your magic feels different. You and I aren't the same."

"Then no, I'm not one."

I rolled my eyes. I wasn't going to get anywhere with this guy.

He assessed me for a long time. "You're awfully young and possess too much magic to fight as you do. Your weapon should be your magic and not the sword."

"Sai, twin sai."

He laughed, and I appreciated the light wispiness of it, the gentle sound that lingered long after he stopped. It reminded me of a wind instrument and the lilting beautiful sound that remained moments after the note stopped.

Shrugging, he dismissed me. "Same thing."

"I had to learn to fight to protect myself out there." I jabbed my thumb near the place that I had come from to enter this place.

"And your parents?"

"Gone." Each time I said it the pang wasn't any less. With each year it seemed like my heart was just as heavy as when I found them. My mouth dried, but at least the tears didn't well like they usually did.

"You do well hiding, but you will not have to for long," he asserted with pride.

I hesitated to ask, because I had a feeling I knew what he was about to say. How many of these so-called maybe I am, maybe I'm not Legacy were there? I slowly shook my head. "Don't." My throat was dry and I forced out a croaky whisper. "Don't." I slowly started to back out. It took nearly a hundred of them to do a spell that killed millions. I didn't know how many there were. How many had he found? How many had been born?

"What's your name?"

"Conner." I wasn't necessarily skilled with the gift of persuasion, but I knew the first thing I needed to do was get to know him. Talk to him and find out about his brand of crazy, because only someone insane or power-hungry would consider this. I also often believed that power hunger was the brutish relative of insanity.

"Conner, you do remember what happened the last time? It was the reason we must hide like fugitives and the world fears us. We got our asses handed to us. Why do it again? Why risk killing us all?"

"A new generation. We've learned from our predecessors' mistakes. They were foolish to do a mass Cleanse when they could have used allies. We will not be so unwise. They were defeated because humans had wielders of magic to help.."

"And the bombs? You might not remember that in others' retelling of this story. Don't glamorize it."

He gave me a faint smile and assessed me, probably the same way I was assessing him. I believe he saw me as a potential ally; I had established he was the enemy. "I don't have to wonder whether the retellings were true, I know what happened. I was there."

I backed away, slowly, trying to get close to the opening of the veil so that I could leave. He extended his hand, holding the sword casually in the other. I wasn't fooled into believing he was innocuous. It would only take seconds for him to be ready to defend. "Come with me, Legacy."

I didn't know if he knew my name and didn't care. He could call me Legacy, but he would never call me ally.

"I'm not going anywhere with you. Let me out."

"I do wish that were possible."

A ball of magic formed in my hand and I thrashed it into the wall. As it had done on the other side, it wavered. How many of them were using their magic to hold it? I threw another, unleashing everything I suppressed into it. Bulging out, almost to the seam, a thinning of the wall. I was about to do that again when Conner lunged at me, making an upward arc with his sword. I moved, turned, and the sai went into him to the hilt. I surged magic through it. He gritted his teeth, and growled.

"Let me out!" I blasted another. He would either throw me out or feel enough pain that he'd wish for death. Or maybe I would do it. "The other one will plunge into a place on you that will be more painful and harder to recover from."

I gripped the sai, yanked it out, turned, and forced all the magic I had in me toward the veil as I ran toward the edge of it. My body burned and tingled as I smashed through it. I tumbled to the ground. Disoriented, I rolled and came to my feet, sai in hand, ready to strike. Panting, I looked up at Savannah, her eyes wide as she stared at me.

"Are you okay?" she asked, but she stayed far from me, a panic-stricken look clinging to her face no matter how much she tried to relax it. I thought it was the blood on the sai, so I looked at them to find that they were as clean as they were before I went past the veil, and so were my clothes. But I didn't feel like I did before I went in. I was a live wire, unused to magic coursing through my body. I stepped away from Savannah. I dropped the twins and touched the tree next to me. Before I could lean against it, it shook, trembled, bark broke off of it, and then it split and then blasted apart, pieces of tree peppering the area. And I thanked the universe for small favors as the magic lingered in the air. So much, but Blu's and that of whichever other witches used the house to perform magic would mask mine.

A calm came over me as I slowly relaxed into myself. The magic bundled up and pushed down again.

"What the hell happened? You've been gone for two hours," Savannah asked, her face more relaxed, although she looked leery as she approached me. Grabbing the sai, I sheathed them and started toward the car.

"I need to talk about it later. We are screwed. So screwed," was all I said.

We almost made it out of the woods. They stretched several more miles than I remembered.

"Olivia," Lucas said as he approached, dressed in a suit. I wondered if he owned any casual clothes. Or did his wardrobe consist of suit, and less suity suit? He wore another dark, tailored suit, peach shirt, handkerchief in his pocket, and cufflinks I was sure could pay my rent for years.

"Why are you trespassing on my property?"

"Your property? This is the witches' property."

He pointed to an invisible line. "They own everything to the right, I own the left side to the streets."

"Sorry, didn't know you owned the woods," I said in a dry voice as I passed him. Fatigue and frustration had made me a little bitchy. I didn't need to take it out on him. "I'm tired."

"You seem like you need rest. Perhaps you should go home and do that and I will meet you"—then he directed his attention to Savannah—"and you as well for dinner."

This again. How many times did someone need to ask before I got a pass to be rude and could tell them, "Shoo. Go away"?

"Have you heard of any more attacks or vampires being controlled?" I asked, making a subtle attempt to change the subject.

"There are very few young ones in our city. The ones that I stopped"—*You mean killed, but please, do go on*—"were the only ones. I've since taken control of the few who are under twenty-five years. They seem to have the most difficulty resisting."

I really wished I knew more about them. For a brief moment I considered taking him up on his offer, if only to find out more about the vampires.

"I assure you, if I am the one controlling their minds, no one else will be able to get to them." Whether he was feeding me lies and false confidence or not, he had definitely put me at ease.

"Thank you," I said, but before I could make it to the car, where Savannah was already sitting waiting for me in the driver's seat, he took me by the wrist.

"Promise you will take me up on my offer." Once again, his voice was like satin slinking over me, a seductively warm and comforting blanket. I became acutely aware of his thumb gliding over my skin in a slow, steady rhythm. I still hoped he was talking about dinner, because he didn't seem like he was. His eyes always went to my neck. Lust and desire cogent in the stare, they spooled in the air between us.

"If you want me to trust you and even consider doing anything like dinner with you, then you're going to have to stop coveting my neck," I stated as he leered at it, whetted with thirst and longing.

He jerked his midnight gaze from it, the silver ring orbiting around his pupils in small beats. "Sorry. I will not deny I have a craving to have it and you."

"Well, that's not remotely better at all."

He smiled and nodded politely. "Then please accept my apologies if I offended you. I do believe in making my intentions known. It makes things less complicated. Despite my desire for you, I will always be a perfect host. You will never have anything to fear. So I do hope you take me up on my offer."

I nodded in agreement, although I didn't plan on taking

him up on that offer anytime soon. Lucas wasn't a man who took rejection, so I could either continue spurning his advances for another half an hour, or agree to consider it but never commit to a time or day. The latter seemed like the easier of the two.

We almost made it. I got to the car. One leg was in when he said, "I will expect you at eight tomorrow. I will send a car for you two." He'd ducked into the passenger side of his Land Rover before I could respond.

That didn't go the way I expected at all.

I sagged into a sigh when I got into the car. I just wanted him to make sure there weren't any more vampire attacks.

CHAPTER 13

a few hours after my run-in with Conner, Kalen waited for us in the living room, coffee in hand and wearing a very haughty satisfied smile as the tart taste of humble pie coated my tongue.

He extended his hands to the chairs across from him and poured us a cup of coffee. After the day I'd had, I wished he'd given me something stronger. I could really go for a shot of whisky; it would at least dull the ache in my body. Or calm the slight vibration that I continued to feel even after destroying that tree. The magic wasn't pumping through my body, but I felt it more now than I'd ever felt it. But I hadn't used so much before, either.

He waited patiently for me to speak and I had a hard time finding the words. When I'd called to ask if Savannah and I could come over to discuss artifacts and ask him some questions, he hadn't hesitated to invite us over.

Several sips later, I started. "Gareth said the Necro-spear is missing, can you tell me about it?"

He took a sip from his cup and relaxed back in his chair, and I realized that we were about to get the extended version of the story. Good. I was sure there would be nuggets of useful information in it.

"It is one of the few objects that can be traced back to magic that is either similar to or is the Legacy magic."

"Similar?" I asked.

He nodded. "Yes, magic from either a Legacy or a Vertu. Although it really doesn't matter, does it?"

"Why is that?" Savannah asked.

"Vertu are considered the originals of magic. All of us can be traced back to some form of their magic. Their closest relatives are the Legacy, who they held dear to their hearts—their children and a direct reflection of the purity of their magic. They are the original magical badasses. It is the accepted belief that they were the ones who were adamant about the Cleanse to ensure that only the purest form of magic existed: them and the Legacy." He frowned and for a moment retreated into his thoughts.

When he finally continued, his voice seemed strained with disdain. "Most accounts of them aren't favorable and quite a few people feared them. If a Legacy was a kill on sight, Vertu were kill on sight, set the body on fire, bury the ashes, set up a ward, and make sure they never came back to life. They were to be feared because of their great power. Even the Legacy couldn't shift, but they could. Into any animal they wanted to without limitation, which made them even more dangerous. They weren't immortal, but trying to kill them, one would think they were."

I looked over at Savannah; she looked pallid. Several times she glanced in my direction. When she finally looked up long enough for me to catch her gaze, she had a look of "why didn't you tell me this?" But I couldn't tell her information I didn't know. Why hadn't my parents told me about them? Had they thought they'd been eliminated and no longer existed? If this was the work of the Vertu, things were worse than I thought.

"They killed hundreds of people, just so they could be the only ones with magic?" Savannah asked.

He nodded. Savannah's color blanched even more as she received a lesson that was never discussed in schools. If Legacy were scary—the Vertu were the ultimate fear.

He continued, "But there were so few Vertu that despite their incredibly great power they didn't consider Legacy their children, but almost their equals. Their allies."

I took another sip of my coffee, my mind drifting to Conner. I didn't think he was a Vertu. He could have shifted to an animal that I had no chance of defeating. I sucked in deeper breaths. Talking about the Cleanse always filled me with grief. My parents' lives changed, others lost their families, and the world as we knew it changed for everyone. History is not quite satisfying when you make it for the wrong reason. I put down my cup. I was clenching it so hard, I was afraid it would shatter.

"Vertu or Legacy, their power was great, and if it weren't for the many mages and witches who came to the aid of the government to get past the veil and shatter the ward, they never would have succeeded. It wasn't strength we had on our side, it was volume. If the Cleanse had worked fast enough, it would have killed the strongest of our kind and we wouldn't have had a chance. It was a quick and bloody two days. A lot of bodies, yet I still don't think we got them all."

My head got a little lighter from holding my breath. I didn't think Kalen would ever tell if he found out, but it would put him in danger, too. Looking at the horror on Savannah's face, I wished I could take back the information, wipe her memory clean. For a brief moment I considered doing it to her—she would be better off. I doubted she would agree to it, and I'd never force it on her.

If they were considering lifting the ban on killing Legacy, Conner and crew were about to make sure they wouldn't.

"You don't think they are all dead?" Savannah asked, peering at him from over the rim of her cup.

"No. It's just too neat. Things are never that neat. Their city was destroyed, but there were tunnels. Vertu could transport and shift. Like fae, they can take on various forms, change appearances. We can't do it for very long and can't make mass, so we can't become someone larger."

Kalen shifted as though he was trying to toss off the dreariness of the story.

"The Necro-spear, can the magic from it be mimicked and harvested? Mages can do that, can't they?" I asked.

The blank look on Savannah's face made me realize I might have been the only one to put it together. Magic working on different frequencies, the reason the Cleanse worked, taking down everyone, witches, mages, fae, vamps, and shifters, because we possessed it all. I kept thinking about what Conner said—allies. Now he had allies. Who would betray their own, and for what? The shifters, witches, fae, and mages found dead at the sites?

I jumped up. "You've helped a lot. I think I know who has the Necro-spear. I'll call you later." He looked startled when I hugged him. I wasn't very affectionate, but I'd figured it out. And it could have been just him talking and allowing the pieces to unfold. I was out of the house before he could ask any more questions.

As soon as we were in the car, I tried to explain everything to

185

Savannah. Her brows furrowed, and she had lost a lot of coloring. It wasn't just the supernaturals who could be affected; humans died, too. Those with dormant supernatural powers who didn't have enough in them to manifest as true magic.

"They thought I was a witch," I said, trying to fill her in after I instructed her to go to the Guild. "When we were attacked at the club, it was just to test blood. My blood. They misidentified me as a witch, because no one knows what a Legacy should feel like. That night in the park, he must have figured out I wasn't a witch." I spoke quickly, but Savannah kept up as she drove through the streets, fast. I would have asked her to slow down but we needed to get to the Guild as soon as possible.

"How did they know that?"

"Because you can't steal our magic. And I bet it was that son of a bitch Conner who wiped my memory."

Now I was pissed I hadn't killed him, but I wasn't sure I would have gotten through the veil without him. Savannah's hands were white from gripping the steering wheel and she had a weird parchment color.

"Savannah, are you okay?" I asked. She shook her head hard.

"Even if the person isn't as strong as you all are and can't do a spell to get the whole world, they can get a city —this city."

I tried to calm her, although I realized nothing I told her was going to help diminish the apprehension. Weathered fear had marked her, and between holding her breath and the color continuing to drain from her face, she looked as if she was ready to throw up.

She let down the window; the wind painfully thrashing her seemed to oddly be what she needed. Ten minutes driving with the window down seemed to settle her into calm. Although the color was missing from her face and her breathing was still short ragged gasps, she seemed better. "So what do we do now?" she asked.

"We need to find and take the Necro-spear. Nothing can be done without it."

"Why you?"

"That was just coincidence. I think." But I wasn't sure and the doubt reflected in my voice. Savannah frowned.

I grabbed my phone and called Gareth, and when he answered I asked, "Do you have any leads on the Necro-spear?"

"No? Why?"

"I need to talk to you. I think I know what is happening. We'll be at your office in about five minutes."

Savannah was in a perpetual state of high alert and walked into the Guild with a dagger clenched in her hand like she was ready to poke anyone who came within six inches of her. She was on edge, and definitely hadn't needed the coffee we had at Kalen's.

"Put the knife away," I said out of the side of my mouth as we walked toward the receptionist, the same woman with the plastic smile. I shook my head; she had a purse on her other arm. *Yeah, you're a stealth assassin with a handbag.*

When she put it in her purse as we neared the elevator, she asked, "What do you think is going to happen to us in the Guild?"

I pointed into the office full of employees. Not one person in there didn't look like life would get a lot worse if anyone dared to cross them. They all looked as if they were just moments from bringing a world of pain.

"We're in a building of supernatural badasses, you're safe."

She scanned the room; her scowl wavered and then turned into a straight-lined frown. "The same 'supernatural badasses' who let the Necro-spear get stolen."

"No, it was stolen from Gareth."

"How is that better?"

"It's not. But the Guild is separate from the Shifter Council. Guild handles all supernatural things. Council handles only shifters."

We'd just gotten off the elevator and headed toward Gareth's office. I was trying to speak quickly and quietly, aware of his acute hearing. I didn't have a chance to finish before he stepped out of his office, arms crossed over his chest as he waited for our approach.

"Ah, Savannah, you've decided that close visual surveillance is the best, I see."

She gave him a polite smile, although based on the little glint of irritation that hit her eyes I knew that she didn't find his statement humorous at all.

"To what do I owe this pleasure?" he asked, directing us into his office. He invited us to sit in the chairs right next to his desk as he sat on the edge of it. Although he seemed relaxed I was aware of tension along his brow and the brackets of his frown.

"When was the Necro-spear stolen?" I asked.

He didn't even have to think about it. "The same day I got it from Kalen." He shifted, watching me with interest, his cool eyes narrowed. I felt like this had changed from a casual encounter to an interrogation. "Why?"

"What do you know about it?" I asked.

He shrugged, frowned. His eyes were still settled on me with avid curiosity and apprehension. I wondered whether he considered me human. I always felt disconcerted when he looked at me, and I felt it even more today.

"If we are pierced by it, we lose the ability to change while in contact with it, and our magical historian states it screws up our immunity to magic."

"Do you know why it does that?" I asked.

"Yes." But he didn't elaborate.

I needed to tell him, but even with the extended drive over here, I couldn't come up with a reasonable story without outing myself. I couldn't tell him about Conner, although I planned on finding that bastard.

"We think someone is trying to do the Cleanse again. Small scale. We don't know why, but they are stealing magic and using the Necro-spear to hold it."

"And you came to that conclusion because?" He raised an eyebrow as his gaze drifted over in Savannah's direction but quickly returned to me. I dropped my eyes. *Dammit. How do I tell him?*

"Have you spoken with Jonathan?"

He looked at his clock. "Just a few minutes ago."

"And?"

Gareth sucked in a breath. "I don't trust that he is innocent in any of this, but I don't have any proof. I can't just accuse him without probable cause."

"But you have cause. There are too many coincidences. Who did the ward on the Necro-spear?"

Again, there was another coarse silence. His was stolid and unreadable. I wasn't sure what was going through his mind, and when he turned to leave, I figured I wouldn't find out. "I need to talk to him again."

I started out after him, behind the four other people he had with him, three of them mages. Stopping at a large SUV parked outside of the Guild, he turned to find Savannah and me right behind him.

"Where are you going?"

189

Before I could answer, Savannah blurted out, "With you all. I want to see you get this jackass. You can't tell me he's not guilty, and after everything he put Levy through, I will not be too hurt if you have to rough him up."

Gareth smiled. "As much as we would love the cheering squad … we can't have one. This might get dangerous."

I opened my mouth to say something and he cut me off. "No, Levy."

We conceded because they could prevent us from getting in the SUV, but they couldn't stop us from following. Or so we thought.

For five blocks we followed them at a distance when two flashing lights and sirens whirled behind us. Savannah looked at the speedometer, confused. When the officer came to the car, she had her license and registration ready.

"I don't need that. Gareth stated you needed to be saved from yourselves, so we decided to intervene. We will be giving you an escort home."

"And if we decline?"

He smiled, his thick jaws ruddy and stiff, but he managed a cool vibrancy in his eyes. "You're not going to do that. Now are you?"

We really wanted to. We really did, but instead, begrudgingly, we took the nice escort home and even the nice surveillance that remained the entire time. Savannah paced, and the attorney's daughter was riled up. Words like *unlawful detainment* came up, *civil unrest*, *abuse of the badge*, and a slew of other things that really didn't seem legitimate or even real words or sayings. More like the rantings of a pre-law student who knew more legal terms than actual definitions.

"I can't believe he did this to us."

I didn't like the role reversal. She was the voice of reason, the logical one. The pseudo–big sister. I liked my role, and now it had to change to calm her down. "You can't believe that he made sure we were out of the way in case things got dangerous?"

"Well, there were three others with him," she huffed, periodically looking out the window at the police cars in front of our building.

"Yes, and at least one of them would have been used to make sure nothing happened to us."

She scoffed. "We can take care of ourselves. And you're like a demigod."

She had taken to calling me that a lot. I really hated that title, although I was willing to give it to Conner. It seemed apropos.

"A demigod who can't do magic in front of anyone," I pointed out.

The realization of it seemed to cool her anger because she stopped pacing and took a seat.

"I'm scared," she finally admitted.

I knew why. If Jonathan was going to do a Cleanse, who would be exempt? People didn't know about their dormant magic until they were dying. Savannah could be one of those people.

I tried to calm her. "We'll know something soon."

It wasn't even soon. Just minutes later Gareth called and told us that Jonathan was gone. His tone was professionally curt and didn't allow room for me to ask questions. Moments after the call, the police escorts left.

Damn. Things were bad.

CHAPTER 14

*J*t might have been my imagination, but the smell of death and blood wafted in the air, the film of magic still there, too. My plans were to never return to the cave and to find a new hiding place, but it still was the closest thing I had to safety, despite both Gareth and Lucas knowing about it. The Necro-spear needed to be found, and I was sure wherever it was, Jonathan wasn't far from it. Find that and the Cleanse couldn't happen, but the tension and fear were there, tightly bound around me like a cocoon. How many Legacy and Vertu remained? I needed to know. Once I found the Necro-spear I would have to find the veil again and find out. But I was working on a lot of assumptions, one being that they would all be in there. What if they scattered, forming alliances all over the world so that they could slowly do it again, this time making sure it was effective? I shook off the thoughts because I needed to focus.

Pricking my finger with a sai, I watched the blood well and fall onto the ground. I did my invocation, pulling from everything I'd learned that had gone unused for so long. My breathing came slow at first as I scanned the area, feeling all the variation and frequencies of magic that weren't my own. It would be the same. Flurries of colors, each one showing the ones different than mine. Piece by piece I wandered the city. It had to be close. It had to be.

Breathing came harder as I became acutely aware of everything: the minute sound of the dirt that settled under my feet, the smells that lingered, residual magic left behind the last time I was here, streams of other magic moving through. And then I saw it. Just the Necro-spear. My head pounded. I didn't know why the feel of the magic was so potent it felt like I was there. It was being prepared, spells chanted over it. Dammit, it was about to be used.

I hopped out of the cave and ran to my car, grabbing my phone and starting the car at the same time. "Gareth, you're going to have to trust me on this. They are about to try it now. You will need to bring mages and witches with you. They will have to bring down a ward." I increased my speed, driving down the long road near Lancing Territory, an area more concentrated with supernaturals than any other part of the city.

I drove up to the abandoned area, the magic so strong it inundated and flooded my senses. I sent Gareth a text with the address and then got out of the car. I was confident I could bring the wards down. But was it just Jonathan in there? I didn't think I could go up against Conner *and* Jonathan. But I was comforted by the fact that he considered Jonathan an ally. He had put his trust in him to do this while he hid behind a veil, safe from being affected by the spell, although I wondered if he could be.

Ten minutes passed and no one showed up. I got out of the car and approached the gray building. Thick doors that I was sure were secured by a board and very durable locks. The small windows weren't low enough for me to reach. As I slowly walked around the barrier, it prickled at me, warm and strong, brushing against the hairs on my arm. My options were slim, but revealing who I was didn't seem so important when thousands of lives were on the line. Sai in hand, I called the magic, a warmth that started and extended through the sai. It shredded the ward. Another strong blast and the doors broke open. Magic blanketed the air, thick and powerful. Jonathan stood in the middle of the room, to his left three men dressed in the same black pseudomilitary gear as the men from HF. My eyes darted over the faces of the men in the room, and one stood out—Clive. This was the big thing he'd been talking about. He'd made a deal with the creatures that he thought shouldn't be near humans to ensure that it happened.

They came at me at once. The first lunged, but not fast enough; the sharp front kick caught his nose, blood spurted. He stumbled back, eyes watering from the fresh break. I hit it again with the butt of my sai and spun to level a side kick into his ribs. I felt the bones give under the impact, and he buckled to his knees and sucked in a ragged breath. Someone punched me in the jaw, hard. My head snapped to the side, the pain shrieked in my jaw. I had to move it to make sure it wasn't broken. Before he could land another blow, I jammed the sai up, ripping through abdominal tissue. He wailed, and I grabbed an arm and with a hip toss threw him on his back. The other guys attacked from each side. A quick turn and they folded when the sai plunged into them. I heard invocations, and magic flooded into the room, turbulent and strong. Each second that passed it came harder and harder, overwhelming the space.

I was quickly making my way toward Jonathan when Clive said, "Levy, stop." I kept advancing until I heard the click of a gun. "I said stop. Don't make me."

I stared into the barrel of the gun trained on me, wondering if I could use magic to disarm Clive. His stern look showed that he knew how to use it and wasn't afraid to. "Drop your weapons, please."

Well, since you said please. But I didn't. I scanned the area—Jonathan was distracted, scared, trying to do that spell while looking at the bodies on the floor, wounded and bleeding.

"I'll only ask once more. Your weapons, Levy."

I lowered them to the ground. His eyes were homed in on me, apprehensive. "Now, put your hands behind your head and get to your knees."

I remained standing, my sharp gaze pushing into him. Defiant. When his finger curled around the trigger more, indifference over whether I lived or died covered his face. I lowered myself to the ground and clasped my fingers behind my head.

"Clive, you don't want to be a part of this. How do you know you will not be one of the fallen? Are you willing to bet your life on being wholly human without any supernatural blood in you?" I attempted to reason with him. Perhaps he'd change the direction of the gun from me to Jonathan and stop it.

His expression didn't falter; it was just as hard and severe. "Yes. If I am not wholly human, then I am okay with sacrificing my life for the cause if I become the problem and not the solution."

What? Clive might be a lost cause. It was hard to reason with radical belief, but I couldn't give up on rational thinking. Someone here had to be reasonable and see this for the disaster that it was.

"You should be ashamed of yourself," I said to Jonathan. He looked up, his appearance stern and dismissive.

The scowl waned for just a mere moment. "Are you going to give me a speech about me being a better person? That I owe it to the Council and to my kind to resist? Whether you like it or not, it's going to happen. But I will be spared. I will be given powers beyond my imagination. No, I don't feel shame at all." Cold, cruel eyes fastened on me, filled with a level of power thirst that was scary.

Since I wasn't in the Betrayers Meeting, I wasn't sure what he'd been promised, but I still couldn't imagine it was good enough to warrant betrayal of the Council and the mages. He returned to the spell, but the words were different. He had to start over. Spells can't be interrupted, which is why it was hard to do them in less than optimal environments.

Clive hadn't relaxed his finger off the trigger, and disregard for me cast a hard shadow on him as he scanned the area, looking for his wounded team. "You are a very dangerous woman, Levy." Intrigue and anger laced his words and I wasn't entirely sure how he felt about that. And I didn't think he was, either.

Jonathan must have had the same concern. "You can't kill her."

And that just ensured that he would. Clive's head snapped around in Jonathan's direction. "I do believe you have forgotten your role. I don't answer to—"

I jumped to stand, kicking the arm holding the gun. It wasn't enough to get him to release it, but he stumbled to the right. Before I could kick him again, a hammer-fisted punch landed on my temple. Pain blared and colors flickered before my eyes. When he attempted to aim the gun at me, I stayed close enough to hold it. He punched me in the ribs and swiped my leg, sending me crashing to the ground. I realized I had underestimated and disregarded him as a pretty boy Spy Guy. Without thinking, I shoved a powerful thrust of magic into his chest, and he soared back, crashing into the wall across the room. The gun went off and a bullet sped past me as the weapon dropped a few feet from him.

Wide-eyed, Jonathan looked at me. "Conner was right, there are a few of you among us."

"And no one will ever know," I said, lobbing another ball of magic, strong and deadly, toward him. He put a ward up, strong, but not impenetrable. My magic destroyed the ward, sending him back several feet. I was about to pummel him with another when Conner flashed in, his eyes going to the Necro-spear. Before he could get to it, I snatched it up and took several steps back.

He popped up again, in front of me. I smiled. "It might be magical, but it's still a dagger," I said as I shoved it into his gut. He was silent until I ripped it out. He growled in pain. I wished it were a sword, because in the time it took for me to position for another assault, he had moved back. The wound and pool of blood that had spread over his peach shirt were gone. What was his deal with pastel colors?

He simply grinned as I readied myself to do another shot of magic, the strongest magic I'd sent in his direction. He captured it, the way someone does a ball, holding it and admiring it like an adorable fluffy puppy, and then he shot it back at me. It barreled into my chest, knocking the wind out of me and sending me soaring through the air. I clung to the spear, refusing to lose it. I was flattened against the floor, gripping the Necro-spear so tightly my fingers were numb. These magical butt-kickings were getting a little tiresome. It took a moment for me to climb to my feet. Seconds that cost me, because when I was up, both Conner and Jonathan were gone. I vowed that Conner was going to get more than his ass kicked the next time I saw him.

But I had bigger problems—five injured HF. Clive was unconscious. I could deal with him later, but I had to erase the others' memories.

I started toward one of the scattered wounded bodies when a crowd of armed people came careening through the door, led by Gareth. He'd brought a small army carrying everything from swords to rifles and all the variations in between. And they were followed by some of the most powerful mages, a witch, and Blu.

I looked at the cavalry and moved closer to Gareth, speaking softly and hoping only he could hear. "You do realize you were here to apprehend one person, right?"

His eyes narrowed, and a belligerent glare brushed over me.

I'm probably not nearly as funny as I think I am.

He ordered them to take Clive and his crew out.

Clive was still unconscious when someone cuffed him and with a single hand lifted him up and draped him over his shoulder. Life was easier when you were a shifter.

Injured, the others were handled a little more gingerly, but not by much.

I was still holding the Necro-spear, the blood cleaned from it the way it had been from my sai after I'd stabbed Conner. I wished I knew how to do that spell. Seemed like a party trick that would come in handy often—blood had power and information.

Gareth was in a mood, a really crappy one. Extending his hands, he demanded, "Spear, Ms. Michaels."

Don't say anything smart. Don't say anything smart. "Keep it safe, I don't want to have to track it down again." *Dammit.* I smiled, sweet and cloying. He turned, slowly scanning the area. A low sound emanated, a rumble so deep the hairs on my arm rose a little. *Did he just roar? Kitty's in a bad mood.*

Another crew of people filed in. I assumed the supernaturals' version of CSI. But instead of being equipped with cool bags and equipment, they had the super-senses of a shifter, cognitive powers of a fae, and magical ability of a witch or mage. Before I could grab my sai and leave, someone from supernatural CSI picked one up.

"Wait. You can't keep that."

"It has blood on it."

"Of course it does, I stabbed a couple of people with it."

"Then we'll need to take it with us," he asserted, dismissing me with an offhanded shrug.

Gareth was heading out the door when I followed behind him and said, "I need my sai."

His voice was cool, distant. He kept walking, an iceberg as he continued toward his car. I repeated my request.

"You can retrieve them after our meeting. Please be in my office in fifteen minutes."

He incited a defiant nature in me that I hadn't known existed. But he also had a lot of power, and also my sai, which I really needed. "Can you make it an hour? I really need a shower. I've admitted to the stabbings." I extended my hands to let him get a full view of my shirt. "It's consistent with it." I'd watched enough police procedurals to know that this probably wasn't going to happen. The supernatural world rules were different, but I didn't know by how much. He paused before he got in his car, looking in my direction, a disfiguring frown etched on his face.

He barely moved his head into the nod. "An hour, and don't pull one of your acts of passive aggression by being late. It will not be met kindly."

"That last part was just unnecessary," I mumbled under my breath, stupidly forgetting who I was dealing with. I risked a glimpse in his direction. *Yep, he definitely heard that.*

I simply waved as I walked past the receptionist. I'd been here so much I felt guilty that I didn't know her name. It seemed like I should start greeting her by it, since she always had that smile that really was infectious, so much that I'd felt a little calmer as I walked by. Midway through the hallway, I was actually relaxed. I was calm—too calm. I stopped and glared at her back. Goddamn fae. I wasn't calm and shouldn't be, but thanks to her fae mojo I was relaxed—too relaxed. I needed to be a little alert and sharp because I hadn't come up with a reasonable story to explain most of everything that had happened. The moment Clive and his band of HF followers started talking, it would put holes in the flimsy story I had. I could imagine telling Gareth: *Jonathan planned to perform the Cleanse using the Necro-spear, which he used to hold a bunch of magic that allowed him to mimic Legacy magic. But don't you worry your pretty little head about that, because it would only be on a small scale. Not a pandemic. By the way, did I tell you there's a couple of Legacy rolling around, and I think Conner is a Vertu? No, that's not a Legacy. He's just their badass daddy. Of course they want to have a Cleanse again, but they plan on rolling it out and beta testing it here. But don't worry, Mr. Cave Lion, there aren't enough to actually do a global spell, so they are outsourcing. Now all they have to do is find more people willing to betray their kind, like Jonathan, with the hope of more power.*

I was so screwed.

When I walked into Gareth's office, he glanced up at the clock and so did I. I was just under the wire by about a minute. I reached for my sai, which were placed next to him. His hand shot out to stop me, then he directed me to the chair in front of his desk.

"You don't trust that I will stay after I have my belongings?"

He chuckled, a roaring sound with haunting amusement. "Oh, you'll stay. But it is probably best that it's on amicable terms."

I inhaled, searching for a calm similar to the fake one Ms. Happy Fae had induced me into earlier. I didn't need to fight with Gareth, nor did I want to. I decided to be the adult in the room.

"Ms. Michaels—"

"Levy."

"Ms. Levy Michaels."

He's not making adulting easy at all.

He inhaled, a faint smile replacing the scowl. "You changed your shampoo. I like it better."

Hmm. And we're going to make it creepy, too. Great.

"Can you tell me what happened?"

I gave him a detailed and very edited version of what occurred, leaving out any magic involvement, although if they interviewed Clive and partners, they would not corroborate it. But it would leave reasonable doubt, and that was exactly what I needed. I told him about Conner, but he was that guy we called a stranger who showed up and helped Jonathan escape.

"What happens to Clive and the others?" I asked, trying to redirect Gareth. He was deep in thought as though he was analyzing my story, assessing it for plot holes and inconsistencies. There were probably a ton of them.

He picked up one of the sai, twirling it with graceful movements of his wrist. He handled it as if it wasn't his first time. If it was, I was feeling like I needed to improve my skills.

"Because they didn't attack a supernatural, we don't have a chance of keeping them here. They will be transferred to the pedestrian system with a full report of your statement." He took his eyes off the swirling sai that was entertaining him and his gaze fell on me, where it stayed. "Unless you have information otherwise."

I shook my head and stepped closer to the desk to retrieve my sai. I grabbed the one on the desk and reached for the one he had. My hand rested over his, waiting for him to transfer it to me. Instead of releasing it, he stepped closer. I inhaled his scent, a wispy earthy and oaky spice. *Oh damn, I'm creepy, too.*

We stood there for a few moments. Me ever aware of his presence as he towered over me. Mesmeric cool crystalline blue eyes fastened on mine. His other hand lightly brushed my hand, his thumb grazed mine. I couldn't squash the desire to feel his lips on mine again. It was carnal, pure hedonism, born from animalistic urges that his shapeshifter magic ignited in me. A roiling attraction that transitioned into an undeniable spark. It was just that magic, his primordial beast connecting with me on a level that was different—inevitable. That was what I tried to convince myself. I pshawed the logic that pointed out that I had encountered several other shifters and hadn't felt anything like this. Not one time did I envision them naked and wrapped around me, but that was all I could think about with Gareth.

He kissed me. Warm, soft lips covered mine. Finally, he released the sai to me, fisting my shirt and pulling me closer. The kiss became more fervent, and when it ended, I leaned into him, wanting more.

It took a moment for my breathing to drop to normal. The hand holding the sai relaxed at my side.

"What are you doing tonight?"

"I have plans," I lied.

Nothing planned, although I knew I would spend most of it thinking about Jonathan and Conner. They didn't have the Necro-spear anymore, so doing a micro-Cleanse was out of the question. And even if I didn't have that to do, I wasn't going to make plans with Gareth.

I didn't say anything for a while, because if I'd opened my mouth I would have said that and agreed to anything he was offering. But I couldn't, because he was still Gareth, head of the Supernatural Guild and a member of the Magic Council.

With the Vertu, possibly a cadre of Legacy, and a treacherous back-stabbing mage on the loose trying to do the Cleanse all over again, the last thing I needed to do was cozy up to Gareth.

I started to back out of the room, and I finally pulled my eyes from his.

As if he knew how much I didn't want to decline, he grinned. "Fine. Maybe another time."

I nodded, still refusing to speak because the lips that were planted on his just moments ago would surely betray me.

Just as I backed out of the door, he called, "Of course, you will not be dealing with this case anymore, right, Ms. Michaels?"

I beamed. "Of course, I wouldn't think of it."

Briskly I walked down the hall. It was hard to leave, but I needed to slow down enough to give the mojo fae a dirty "I know what you did to me" look. And I did, and she shot me a very pleasant smile that was punctuated with a look of "And?" Or it could have been, "My boss made me do it." Who was I kidding? I didn't know what her looks said. I couldn't read looks.

CHAPTER 15

*T*hings were really terrible when you were happy that things were just *less bad*. And that pretty much was where I was. Gareth had the Necro-spear. I doubt it would be stolen again, but there were still people who wanted to do a Cleanse. I couldn't help but wonder—if they could have used the Necro-spear to do a Cleanse, how many more Legacy objects were out there? Instead of going home, I pulled over and made a call to Kalen. I needed my KUI. I needed to change that nickname because he'd effectively no longer provided useless information. His information was quite useful.

Kalen was exceptionally self-satisfied when he answered the door, dressed more casually than I had ever seen him, in a dark t-shirt and jeans. When I walked in farther, I noticed four large boxes on the floor. He handed me a bottle of water and waved his hand near a spot on the floor. "We'll work and talk."

Starting on the box next to me, he asked, "What can the KUI do for you?" He shot me a dirty look and the heat of embarrassment rose over my cheeks. With a crooked grin, he teased, "Didn't know I knew that, did you?"

I busied myself going through a box, pulling things out and separating them into categories as we always did. "I have no idea what you are talking about," I said innocently.

"Of course," he said, flicking water on me.

I laughed. "You know I'm only going to take so much of this mistreatment before I leave you. Maybe I'll apply for a position at the Guild, they seem to pay okay. You should see Gareth's home."

"I don't think they hire humans, even a cantankerous, smart-mouth malcontent like yourself." He grinned. "So you've been over to Mr. Gareth's house? Do tell."

I brushed it off with a wave and a wry smile. "Nothing to tell. I was attacked by shifters, bloody, and I went to his house to shower."

He gave me a doubtful side glance. "And?"

"And nothing. His home is gorgeous."

"It should be. Do you know how much he's worth?"

"Nope, but I know how supercilious and officious he can be."

I ignored the look of utter reproach that he gave me. "His mother is Jennifer Chase-Reynolds. You know, the woman who owns our cable company, three malls"—he gave me another one of his looks of reproach, appraising my outfit —"you might want to visit one and fix this." His open palm did a dramatic wave over me from head to toe as his lips bent into a disappointed frown at my oversized blue button-down shirt, jeans that might have seen their last year of wear, and my favorite pair of blue Converses.

Jumping to my feet, I did a spin, cocking my head back and assuming my best model pose. "It's retro chic. But I understand that your simple sensibilities can't appreciate my avant-garde fashion," I responded in a playful, haughty tone before plopping back on the floor next to the box. I didn't want to talk about Gareth or my wardrobe. I needed answers.

He rolled his eyes. "And I will not even discuss her other real estate."

Then why did Gareth even work? Was he drawn to the danger? Was he that addicted to power? I didn't have time to discuss Gareth. He wasn't a priority. I needed to find Jonathan and Conner, and not necessarily in that order.

"Mages, what do you know about them?" I asked, changing the topic.

He stopped poking around in another box and looked straight forward, his mouth twisted and his brow furrowed in thought. "What do you need to know? The history or their magical capabilities?"

"Gareth said it was rumored that mages have necromancer abilities, is it true? Can they control vampires?"

He nodded. "They can perform the dark arts, but most of them are afraid to."

"Why, is it illegal?" I asked.

"It's not if they aren't using it for nefarious reasons, but if they are using it to control vampires, it is. And it is very draining on their powers and can take days to recover from. Most supernaturals do not like being weak, vulnerable. Why do you ask?" He went back to rifling through the box, pulling everything out of it. I was always amazed that people just shoved everything in a box and sold it. But it was our business and it worked out well. Some of it was junk, or so I considered it, like the Atari system he pulled out of the box. And some not, like a first edition of Keats. I couldn't believe it came from the same household. And then he pulled out a large pewter-colored stone. I could feel the magic on it. We only got things like this from humans—they couldn't sense the magic. It was a Hearth Stone, one witches used to pull in magic from their ancestors. Very valuable. I would probably call Blu and offer it to her first. I felt like I owed her.

"Because I think it was a mage who was responsible for Savannah and me being attacked at Crimson. And that same mage tried to do his version of the Cleanse yesterday."

Kalen's eyes widened as he pushed his box aside and then moved mine. "Enough of work! What?"

So I had to give him the condensed modified version I gave Gareth, leaving out all the parts about me doing magic. I was looking forward to seeing Savannah so I could finally talk about the whole unedited version of this story.

"He murdered seven people in order to do that Cleanse. Why? Why would he do such a thing?"

"I think he was bribed," I offered. I knew he had been bribed. Utter disgust and contempt melded over Kalen's face at the betrayal. "And the man who saved him, I think was a Legacy or maybe even a Vertu?" I hoped he didn't ask any follow-up questions, because I hadn't perfected a story that would explain why I knew this bit of information.

As the anger and disgust faded, leaving behind a very portentous air, he sighed several times. "No one knows how many magical objects were taken. They've never been fully cataloged. The Magic Council has some, but what about those that were probably lost in transition or even pillaged?"

My parents often spoke of their history, but as I recounted the many things they'd told me, I couldn't remember any specifics about magical artifacts. Most of it had to be relegated to the back of my mind, stored with the memories of my parents, because they all brought the same pain that I had grown tired of dominating my life and reliving almost on a daily basis. "I assume the Cleanse required a great deal of magic, very hard to replicate, which is why he needed the Necro-spear. Magic is magic, as you've said a thousand times before. At its very essence and core"—I stopped, and he probably thought it was a dramatic pause or to gather my thoughts, but I almost said "we," including myself—"you all are the same but manifest it differently, right? I don't think it can work without all the pieces that make up the core of magic's existence. I'm not saying you shouldn't be nervous; as long as the Necro-spears are available, there is a possibility. But we know the pattern, and only a small number of people can do it. The Guild is aware, and I am confident they can stop it even if someone chooses to try."

In my effort to comfort Kalen, I claimed a piece of it for myself. I still wanted to kill Jonathan, then find a necromancer to raise him from the dead so I could kill him again. And I wanted Conner dead so badly I ground my teeth at the mention of his name or anytime I thought of him. I would have to find all the Necro-spears, and it would help if I knew how many.

He nodded, with a renewed curiosity. "How do you know so much about this?"

"Everyone keeps mistaking me for a witch; I think I might have a link to them." It was kind of sort of the truth. "So if a Cleanse happens, I will probably be affected, too." That was the truth. I would die with everyone else; we were spared initially because we were secured behind an impenetrable ward that protected us while the world crumbled outside of our own magical one.

"I have to go; I will be in tomorrow."

"Yeah, well, I'll make sure to add the whole fifteen minutes of work you did to your paycheck," was his snarky response from behind me as I headed out the door.

"More like thirty minutes. And hazard pay for spritzing me with water. I could have drowned."

His robust laugh filled the air, and honestly I needed it. The weight of the world was still there, and although I'd only given Kalen a mere piece, edited and repackaged, I still felt better. I looked forward to unweighting myself more with Savannah.

I approached our apartment door, holding the twins tighter. I could feel the magic that dampened the air. My heart raced and regulating my breathing became impossible. Our front door was slightly open. I eased in, and the magic washed over me. Jonathan. The table was knocked over, the television cracked and on the floor. Savannah's favorite chair on its side. I called her name in a strained dry croak, knowing I wouldn't get an answer. But I still looked, hoping I was wrong. Maybe she was hiding somewhere. I checked the closets, under the bed, any place a person her size could hide.

Fuck. They had taken Savannah.

Scanning the area, I looked for a note or something and came up short. What type of bastard left nothing? Jonathan, that was who, because the egotistical bastard knew I'd know it was him. When I picked up my phone, I had a message from Savannah with an address. And a simple message: "Leave it there."

I called Gareth and as soon as he picked up, I said, "They took Savannah."

He cursed into the phone, and I was glad I didn't have to explain anything with my gravelly trembling voice that was just moments from breaking. The tears welled, more so out of anger than anything else. I was teeming with a level of rage that was new for me, and I didn't know how to subdue it. Vengeance rode me hard. Gareth's commanding voice broke me out of it.

"I can't give them the Necro-spear for Savannah, Levy," he said. "Let me—"

I hung up. I knew that wasn't going to happen and I wasn't sure why I'd called him. I could track Jonathan, but I needed something of his. He'd touched the Necro-spear, but that wasn't enough. I needed more. Something intimate—blood, clothing, hair, a possession that was uniquely his. The anger and thirst for revenge made it difficult to stay on task, but the phone ringing pulled me out of my thoughts.

"Don't you hang up on me again," Gareth's commanding voice roared through the phone. *Definitely a lion.*

I didn't have time to fight with Gareth. I mumbled an apology.

"I have four mages working on tracking him. Come to the Guild as soon as you can. We will find her, okay?"

"Thank you." But before he could hang up I had to ask, "How? Do you have anything of his?"

"Yes, his blood. It's a Council requirement, and it's a good thing for times like this. It was done to help track us if we ever went missing, usually in a kidnapping situation, but …"

My lungs relaxed into the exhale. *This is what breathing feels like.* The restricted feeling had gone away. "I will be there in a few minutes," I said, then added, "Good-bye," remembering him barking at me about hanging up on him. He'd earned my compliance.

I locked our front door and turned to find Lucas just inches from me. Startled, I took a step back. Definitely didn't like that about vampires.

"What's the matter?" he asked with concern.

"Savannah's missing," I said, sidestepping by him to get to my car.

Grabbing hold of my arm, he turned me to face him. "What?"

"She's missing. I have to be at the Guild. I really don't have time to explain everything to you." I rushed out and made another fruitless effort toward my car.

"If time is of the essence, I can get you there faster." He guided me toward the motorcycle parked in front of the apartment. I looked at my Focus, which I wasn't quite sure would start. Most times it was hit or miss, and she was definitely slower than a motorcycle would be. But I couldn't help but wonder who rode a bike in a suit. *Okay, this time it's not a suit.* He had on a simple black dress shirt, cuffed to the forearm. We got on the bike and I wrapped my arms around him. As soon as I did he started down the street.

We zoomed through the city. I buried my face into his back, closed my eyes, because seeing the world at a blur was making me sick. He might get me to my destination faster, but I wasn't sure if it was going to be in one piece. When he pulled up in front of the Guild, I jumped off the bike, and we rushed into the building. My phone had vibrated in my pocket for the second time. I pulled it out and saw that it was Gareth, but at the same time he was getting off the elevator. As he made his way down the hall, he was joined by five other officers. Harrah was nearly jogging to keep in step with him.

"Gareth." Her voice was gentle and urgent as she kept pace with him. "You have to end this as quickly as possible. Today you will be expected to give a press conference. You know a rogue Magic Council member is going to look terrible. Don't mention anything about a Cleanse because that hasn't been confirmed and there isn't a need to alarm anyone."

His face was nearly expressionless, but his voice was razor-sharp. "Harrah, I heard you the first two times. Public image is the last of my worries right now. I need to apprehend a murderer and abductor. I don't care how it plays out in the court of public opinion."

But Harrah did, because it was her job to. She placated the pedestrians and made magic seem harmless.

"I'll do the press conference, but if you expect me to play nice, I'd suggest you do it yourself," he growled.

Her arms were crossed over her chest as she stopped in the middle of the hallway. Gareth kept walking. I wanted to give her the benefit of the doubt; she was working in the best interest of the community. She wasn't as cold as she seemed until she said, "If you are sure he's guilty, I don't want him kept alive. We will develop the optics for it. I need to address it so that the humans continue to trust us—and not consider us dangerous. This is a problem and it needs to be handled. *He* needs to be handled."

My head jerked in her direction. I'd suspected that gentle facade was her best foot forward. I didn't realize it was an all-out mask that hid a person who was ruthless and pragmatic when it came to maintaining the public image of the supernatural community. I wondered how many times things had been handled in this manner. Ice crawled up my spine as I realized that I would be handled just as callously and practically if I were discovered. I tried not to look back at her, but I couldn't help it. Everything about her was as gentle and calm as a meandering stream—except her eyes, which held the dark shadows of malice and mercilessness.

When Gareth simply nodded at her request, the ice turned to tension that seized my body. It was that sliver of hope that if he found out about me, he would be understanding. But he was still in command of the SG and that was where his commitment and alliance lay. I wasn't mourning Jonathan's life, he deserved to die. He'd killed seven people out of thirst for more power. There wasn't a place for sympathy for him. But it added to the fears I had about being discovered. The nightmares of people finding out and seconds later I was a puddle of blood on the ground, not even given a moment of consideration that I might deserve to be spared.

Lucas seemed just as surprised as I was when Gareth gave him the address in passing as he got into his car. Someone got into the passenger side and the rest into a department-issued sedan, similar to police cars except they were black and the lettering was dark, barely visible, which I think was the point.

Pressed against Lucas's back, I felt weird not hearing anything: breathing or heartbeat. But that probably wasn't such a bad thing because I was breathing hard enough for both of us and my heart was racing as he careened down the street, weaving in and out of traffic, my surroundings reduced to nothing but blurs of colors and whizzes of sound.

We got to the little cottage nearly an hour away, in the middle of a bare field. Stretches of just grass and nothing else. Magic was thick and glazed the air. The power of it pumped hard.

Within a few feet of it, we crashed into the ward. Lucas pushed harder into it and it rebounded with equal force, throwing him back several feet. Jonathan stepped out of the house onto the porch, his lips twisted into a cruel smile. I stood inches from it, meeting his gaze.

"Give her to me."

"Do you have the Necro-spear?" He stepped closer to the ward as he shot me hateful glares. "If you ruin this for me, I will kill her and then you."

Gareth approached the ward with two mages at his side. Magic illuminated off their hands, the push striking the ward. It wavered but stood. They wouldn't bring it down, because it wasn't his magic. And if it was, it was enhanced by Conner's. Then Jonathan stepped away, moving back into the house. One glance back and a wolf soared, clawing into one of the Guild mages' back, blood splattering as it ripped at his flesh. Its eyes were wide and blank, its acts controlled by someone else. It started for the other mage. Before I could move, Lucas flashed past me, charging the wolf; his hand gripped around its neck as he sent it crashing onto its back on the ground. He was about to break its neck when I yelled, "Please don't. He's being controlled."

He hit it once and then again and several more blows until it stopped moving. It was unconscious, but better that than dead.

Four more animals came out, padding fast. Gareth ran toward them, shifting midstride into the massive lion that charged them, his paw striking, sending them back. Lucas took on another wolf. The other SG officers had guns. I looked again. I thought they were tranquilizers. That lifted some of the guilt. I had a problem with people dying for something they had no control of. It was just too close to home.

The remaining mage was still working on the ward. I walked around, getting lost in the chaos. The sai in hand, I pulled magic, just as much as I needed to shatter the magical wall. Remnants of its existence floated in the air. I ran into the house; Jonathan was on one side of the room, Savannah on the floor. Her eyes were closed, and I watched, waiting for her to breathe. *Come on. Savannah, please.* Her chest rose, but barely. I was able to exhale before the charge of magic thrashed into my chest, sending me crashing into the wall, the sai tumbling out to the side. I jumped, reaching for them, but I was struck by something sharp in my ribs. Jonathan had kicked me. Hard. He was past anger, reduced to a madman, enraged as he watched the life he'd been guaranteed slip through his deceitful fingers. He attempted another kick. I whipped around on my butt, swiped his leg. When he crashed down next to me, my elbow crushed into his windpipe. He gasped for breath. He pushed a wave of magic, and I stumbled a couple of feet and waved it away. I'd grabbed the sai, ready to end it, when Lucas moved past me. One second

Jonathan was struggling for breath, the next his neck was wrenched into an odd angle; he was breathless and unmoving.

Before I could fully grasp what had happened, he was next to Savannah, his fingers pressed to the pulse in her neck...

CHAPTER 16

*S*avannah in Lucas's arms was the last thing I saw before I disappeared. Conner held me secured against his chest, where I most likely would have stayed if I hadn't pulled away. I held the sai at my sides, gripping them, thumbs ready to flick off them. I had them perfectly positioned to strike.

"Anya, please relax."

I stayed in position. He smiled, kind and disarming, and for a brief moment I could see how one could be swayed by the charismatic stranger. "Anya Kismet. You've abandoned it for so long that it is foreign. It means nothing to you." A hint of sadness accompanied his words. He reached out to grab my hair and I blocked it with the side of the dull shaft of the blade. With a wry smile he pulled his hand back. "You changed your hair."

I'd been brunette for so long, I'd forgotten that Legacy hair was red—not just red, but fiery persimmon. A dead giveaway. The palest to the darkest of our kind, we were cursed, or blessed, depending on who was describing it, with the same color hair. Our crown that let everyone know who we were.

I lifted my eyes to his dark brown coif. "Hypocrisy much?"

"Yes, I must blend with the insipid as well." He ran his finger through his hair, changing it to its natural color. It fit him. I don't think I'd ever seen my natural color.

He looked at my hands and rolled his eyes. "Please, Anya, relax your weapons. I will not hurt you, I give you my word."

"Then I will not hurt you, either," I said, placing them back in the sheath.

He chuckled, finding humor instead of the ire I had infused in my words.

"Why am I here?" I asked, looking over the fallow land. The small patches of grass were barely alive. The barren land stretched for miles. There were only four small, simple white cottage-style homes. Nothing like the extravagance my mother spoke of when she described where she grew up and lived. Empyrean was what the Legacy had named their little town, Heaven, fifty miles from the border of the city, miles and miles of unused land to separate them from the others. The supernaturals they considered beneath them and the humans that they held little to no regard for at all. She spoke so fondly of the palatial homes, the magically enhanced grassland, exotic flowers that climbed and wrapped around the rails of the gates at the entrance of Empyrean and that extended out miles before you entered the town. The barrier that separated them from everyone else. People would travel to Empyrean just for a look at them, even though they would never gain entrance to the city. This wasn't the nirvana I expected.

He stared at me for a moment, then looked over his shoulder, seemingly taking in the dire backdrop from my perspective. "I see my living quarters aren't up to your standards. Since there are so few of us, and this place is simply temporary, we didn't exert great efforts, just provided ourselves with the basics."

A smile spread over his face, brightening his eyes and his voice. "Please, let's walk and talk." I stood, rooted in my spot. I didn't want to do that and get farther from the veil.

"I don't need to be awed by the beauty of your home; you can impress me with honesty. Why are you doing this?" I asked.

He started to walk, but I stood my ground.

He sighed. "Anya, this is your new home, please give up any thoughts of leaving." He extended his hand. "Please, walk with me."

"I'm not staying here."

Smile diminishing, he said, "I will satisfy your curiosity, and in return I expect you here by my side."

"Why don't you just tell me whatever information you are willing to offer that will allow me to leave once the conversation is over?"

He tilted his head, but he didn't possess any more humor. It had drained from his face and his words. "I'm sorry if I gave you any impression that you would be able to leave. That isn't going to happen. I'm glad you had the chance to see Savannah before you left, because you are here to stay."

Like hell I am. I thought I'd only said it in my head.

He exhaled an exasperated breath. "I will have to take over your mind and control your actions and make sure that you don't. I'd rather you stay and follow of your own volition, but I will do it if necessary. I am stronger than you are. You may challenge, but you will fail."

"Like you did with the vamps and shifters?"

"The shifters only. Jonathan took care of the vampires, although he was reluctant to practice the darker arts. I guess the reward of more power and status was worth the risk."

He started to walk, knowing my curiosity would force me to follow. As I did, flowers bloomed from the tree he'd just created. He pulled off one and handed it to me. I stared at it. He frowned at my refusal and let the flower fall. It disappeared before it hit the ground.

His tone was soft and wistful. "It wasn't supposed to be this way. Jonathan thought you were a witch, and when he found he couldn't take your magic, he called me."

"And you just left me there to take the fall for three murders?"

"Yes," he said in an even voice, as though he wasn't telling me that he'd set me up to be exposed and possibly murdered. "I did not believe you would have been found innocent." He frowned. "When I find a sliver of hope and respect for them, they always disappoint."

"I'm happy they disappointed you and I actually got out of the place alive. But don't let that concern you."

Conner stopped and turned to me. "I wouldn't have let you stay in there. But your allegiance would have been to me. Loyalty is earned. If I would have saved you from certain death, I would have earned that from you. You would be more acquiescent than you are now. The three who I have now are loyal to me because I've earned it. I will earn yours as well."

"There are three more, where?"

"Two have been sent out to recruit more."

"Can I meet the other one?" I needed to see their faces at least and know who I was dealing with.

"In time you will meet them all."

Clasping his arms behind him, he started to walk. He slowed as he realized I hadn't followed. I looked back at the entrance; I was nearly twenty yards away. I didn't want to go any farther. My thirst for knowledge outweighed my caution. I followed, walking slowly, forcing him to ease his steps to stay close. I got the impression he wanted to talk as much as I wanted the information.

"Why should we be relegated to hiding in fear and forced to live behind veils? I want to live as we did before."

"Legacy and Vertu lived behind veils before," I countered.

"Because we wanted to, not because we had to. I will not live like this."

"We live in hiding because of the horrible shit we did before. Our kind killed people. Have you not learned from their mistakes?" I tried to stay calm, but I couldn't and found that I was yelling at him. That wasn't going to work. Diplomacy was needed. Mastering my anger, when I spoke again, my tone was soft and level. "If you go through with this you will make things worse, not better. Learn from your descendants' mistakes."

"But I have learned from their mistakes. They were foolish to try something so global—it used too much of their power and made them weak when it was time to fight. Many escaped, and for years we've procreated, in hiding, producing more than have been killed. People like Jonathan and his ilk will help us. Small Cleanses, until the supernatural world is weaker, and then we strike it. It is not a short-term plan that I'm looking at. Things will be better than ever before. We will be stronger, something that exceeds everything they ever created or dreamed of."

What type of demagogue shit is this?

I made another attempt at reason. "I'm … *we* are forced to hide what we are, change our hair, have shields tattooed on us so that we can live a somewhat safe life so we aren't hunted by Trackers or discovered by the Supernatural Guild, and your answer is to do that very thing that made us pariahs among the supernaturals and our kind."

His stern look of obstinacy made me realize there wasn't anything I could say that would persuade him otherwise.

"I'll stop you."

"My warrior mate. I believe it is wise that I waited for a good pairing. We will make a good couple, and we will rule well together because people will respect us. Our children will have an impressive lineage. A Vertu and Legacy."

"I'm sorry? What?" I had missed something. "What do you mean 'our children will have an impressive lineage'? Because it sounds like you consider me a broodmare, and that isn't going to happen."

"I consider you no such thing! But you are a thoroughbred who will make beautiful, powerful children. I'm glad I waited. You will be an adequate consort."

I scoffed. "I'm not letting you anywhere near me."

Thin, supple lips lifted into a charming half-smile. "I find it odd that you reject me when so few women are able to do so."

"Try telling them you plan on killing off half the world, that sure will knock the shine off your luster."

He dismissed it with a wave. "We have two impressive Legacy women whom I could have chosen. I'm glad I waited, because I feel a connection with you."

"It's called *disdain*, not a connection," I offered. "One, you and I aren't going to happen because you desire it. Two, there is no way in hell I'm letting this happen. I will stop you."

"I'm quite sure you will try. I hope you choose to be at my side, willingly as my consort, my better half. I would rather have a partner and a confidante who will be with me as I accomplish my lofty goals. If I must control your mind the entire time, I fear that I will break you. I don't desire to have a broken woman at my side."

"Then you'll break me, because that is the only way you will have me."

"Anya, don't fight this. I've broken stronger and persuaded those far more stubborn than you."

"There is no power in your persuasion, just flaws in the plan. The ones you've so-called broken or persuaded have sold their souls for power. And just as they have betrayed their own, they will do the same to you."

Frustrated, he blew out another breath. "I loathe that you consider me stupid and my intentions cruel. There is civility in what is being constructed. Humans First and I have the same goal. Separation of the two."

"I'm sorry but I *loathe* that I can wade through your BS and see the truth. You don't want separate but equal. Those supernaturals who betray their own to help you will have a place. The others will be dead. Meaning if you ever decide to pull any crap, you can hide behind a ward and be untouchable by the humans. They will not be living in harmony; if they have any sense, they will be living in fear."

Talking to him wasn't going to help. I had to put the fire out at the base. He was the leader, the head of the movement. Stop him and I would be given time to stop the others while they mobilized and regrouped. I could do this.

I snatched out the sai and plunged one in his gut, invoking a spell as I tried to block him from healing. I needed him weak enough to fade the veil. He was right— magic to magic, he'd kick my butt. We'd established that. I jabbed him in his throat with the other. He gasped out for air. And did it again. He started to choke. I wasn't going to lose any sleep if I killed him. I pulled out the sai and kicked him back. He didn't go as far as I'd like, but I'd take what I could get. I ran toward the veil, the magic welling inside of me. It was strong, rising in me in waves. A tsunami of magic ready to be expelled. I planned to force it all into the veil. As I got closer I could feel the strength of Conner's magic. He might have been injured, but the veil was still strong. *I got this.* I hoped I had it. With sai in hand, I hoped Conner's blood on them would help. My confidence that it would wasn't very high. I was winging the hell out of this, but I shoved them where I thought the barrier started, forced magic into them, and ripped it open. A wave of magic, Conner's magic, hit my back as I fell through the opening, crashing facefirst into the ground. I didn't care. I was outside the veil. Home. Okay, not home, but on someone's land eating dirt. And I was happy to do it.

Get up, I commanded myself. But I couldn't. I'd drained everything out of me. I had to rest, but I was too close to the veil. Once Conner had healed he could come for me again. I forced myself to stand and stumble forward and had only made it a few more feet before I collapsed again. I closed my eyes for just a few seconds. *That's all that I need.*

"Levy." The deep voice was off at a distance. *Not Anya. Yes, Levy.* I pried my eyes open. "Hey," I whispered to Gareth, who was just inches from me.

"Are you okay?"

"Of course, I always rest facedown in the dirt. It's my thing," I said in a muffled voice.

He sighed lightly. "Yes, that wit, I'm sure someone finds it appealing."

He scooped me up.

"Oh god, don't damsel me. Please let me walk."

"Sure." He lowered me closer to the ground, and when I was a few inches away, he let me drop.

I grunted. "You're an ass."

"I'm too much of a gentleman to call you one back. Are you ready to be *damseled*? Or should I reposition you so that your face is in the dirt the way I found you?"

Feeling his eyes on me, I tried to find the resolve to get up. Couldn't muster even a tendril of it. I was exhausted. My eyes fluttered, trying to stay open.

"You are too damn stubborn for your own good," he said, lifting me. "Say something smart and I will drop you, again."

I worked my lips to say just that, something smart, before I stopped myself. I had worse battles to fight. I kept my mouth shut and pressed my head into his chest as he carried me across the woods to his car. The moment my head hit the leather seats, I fell asleep.

Each time I opened my eyes, he peppered me with questions. Fatigue made it hard to edit the way I wanted to, and that was probably the point.

"His name is Conner and you are sure he's a Legacy?" he asked.

"No, I'm not sure of anything. I'm just telling you what he said." I needed Gareth to have a seed of doubt in my story until I figured out what I was going to do. I was telling him that a Legacy existed. Well, a Vertu. Would it be long before he connected the information?

"Why did he want you?"

"I don't know?" I lied. I closed my eyes, and when he asked more questions, I feigned sleep. The many thoughts were giving me a headache and I was too tired to make any rational decision.

CHAPTER 17

Savannah sat on the bed, one leg bouncing impatiently over the other. Her arms were crossed and she shook her head at another outfit I pulled out of my closet and showed her. I knew she was waiting for me to pull out something similar to her teal single-strap dress that caressed her curves. Her hair was down and cascaded over her shoulders, and her makeup enhanced the glow of a person always hopped up on endorphins. She looked gorgeous. I almost considered joining her cult.

"I can't believe you thought it was okay to wear that. It's fine for going to a community yard sale, but not to have dinner with the Master of the city."

I looked down at my outfit: a pair of burgundy chino pants and a white top. "I would never wear something this nice to a yard sale." Then I grinned and gave her attire a once-over. "And you think it's okay to show so much neck going to dinner with a vampire."

"He's hundreds of years old, I'm sure he's been around hundreds of exposed necks and can control himself."

She leaned over and snatched the plain blue dress I was

about to put on out of my hand and tossed it on the bed. Then she went to the closet and pulled out a black pencil dress with double halter straps and pushed it to my chest. "Now get dressed, he's sending someone to pick us up in less than an hour."

As I undressed and started putting on the dress, I shot her my meanest of glares while she ignored it. "Do you think this is a good idea?" I asked.

"Yes. He saved my life. If he wants to have dinner with us every day of the week, we will do it." I slipped on the dress and a pair of shoes I knew she would approve of. Strappy silver heels. I just didn't want to debate about it, but my comfortable flats really looked more appealing.

"I know, but I have so many things I need to do. I can't pretend what Conner told me didn't happen. I need to do something about it." And I did. But I wasn't going to do anything about it at ten o'clock at night.

It took her a long time to answer. I'd given her little pieces of it after Gareth brought me home. And I slept for over twelve hours, getting up once to get food and then crawling back in the bed to get more sleep. I'd only been out of bed for four hours when I found out she had agreed for us to have dinner with Lucas.

"I know," she said softly. "*We* have a lot of work to do. But tonight, let me not have to relive yesterday, and Jonathan nearly killing me. Or how bad you looked when Gareth brought you home. Or the horrible things you told me today. We'll deal with whatever it is. We will find the Necro-spears if there are any more and locate every Legacy left to warn them or at least figure out whose team they are playing on. I'll even learn to fight with your damn sticks."

"Sai."

She dismissed my offering with an eye roll and a wave of her hand. "Oh, whatever. The sharp stabbing sticks. Tonight let's have a great dinner and expensive wine and enjoy Lucas's amazing tales—he's been alive forever, they have to be interesting. Okay?"

I nodded. "How do you know he's not going to serve us McDonald's and give us a bottle of Two Buck Chuck? Just because he's old doesn't mean he has amazing tales. Maybe he's lived this long because he's dull, and the most exciting thing about him is that he's a vampire."

Sighing in exasperation, she perked her lips into a half-smile. "Whatever will I do with you?" She left me to finish getting dressed. Just as she made it out of the door, she ducked her head back in. "And you better not wrap a scarf around your neck, you'll insult him."

We knew each other too well, because several moments were dedicated to picking out the best scarf for the outfit.

She was gone before I could point out the number of times I had caught him looking at my neck like it was an option on the menu.

When the doorbell rang, I expected Lucas's Suits to be at the door, not Gareth. He took one look at me and smiled. "Is this for me?"

"I didn't know you were coming, how could this be for you?"

He shrugged, peeked past me at Savannah, and back at me. "I don't know, perhaps you saw me walking up to your door and decided to change. If you did, I appreciate it."

"You are arrogant, aren't you?"

He chuckled. "'The lady doth protest too much, methinks.'"

Leave it to Gareth to quote Shakespeare in an insult.

"I can hear your heart rate. Either I really piss you off so

227

much that you can't control yourself, or—well, I guess I don't need to finish the rest." His half-grin was just as gloating as his tone. "And the breathing"—he made a sound with his teeth—"I really get you going, don't I?"

"I don't think any woman will ever think you are as hot as *you* think you are. Why are you here?"

"I was in the neighborhood and wanted to see how you were doing."

"You were in this neighborhood? Why?"

We didn't live in a bad neighborhood, but it was boring and not a lot went on near us. People like Gareth didn't just hang out on this side of town.

He shrugged. "Why not? How are you?"

"Fine."

Silence pushed from seconds to minutes. "I should go," he said. But he didn't move; instead he stood there for a moment. "Thank you for your help with the case."

"You're welcome."

Then he stepped closer. Face-to-face. And when he leaned forward, I closed my eyes, expecting to feel his lips against mine. Instead they brushed against my ear as he spoke. In a breathy whisper, he said, "I enjoyed working with you, Anya Kismet."

He turned and walked away before I could exhale the breath that I held on to the moment he said my real name. Thoughts flooded my mind as I tried to figure out how he had found out and what he was going to do with the information. Sensing the change in my mood, Savannah was next to me in seconds. "What's the matter?"

"He knows who I am," I gasped in a strained whisper.

"Did he say if he's going to say anything or do something about it?" she asked, concerned, her voice just as tight and wispy as mine.

We were both staring at him as he made his way to the

car. I considered running after him and trying to figure out what else he knew. But if he knew my real name, he probably knew for sure what I was. And maybe so much more.

Before he got into his car, he smiled. Then pressed his finger to his lips.

"I don't think he will."

MESSAGE TO THE READER

Thank you for choosing *Double-Sided Magic* from the many titles available to you. My goal is to create an engaging world, compelling characters, and an interesting experience for you. I hope I've accomplished that. Reviews are very important to authors and help other readers discover our books. Please take a moment to leave a review. I'd love to know your thoughts about the book.

For notifications about new releases, *exclusive* contests and giveaways, and cover reveals, please sign up for my mailing list at mckenziehunter.com.

Happy Reading!

www.McKenzieHunter.com
MckenzieHunter@MckenzieHunter.com